Praise for John Ball's *In the Heat of the Night*

"Top-notch, with current sociological implications."
—*Saturday Review*

"This breathtaking suspense novel won an Edgar Award and introduced homicide investigator Virgil Tibbs. Mr. Ball handles the racial situation with detailed perception."
—*The New York Times Book Review*

"It has the excitement and freshness that set it apart . . . this is a genuine classic and makes most other crime stories look dull."
—*The Sunday Times* (London)

Also by John Ball available from Carroll & Graf

The Kiwi Target

In The Heat Of The Night

JOHN BALL

Carroll & Graf Publishers, Inc.
New York

For Reverend Glynn T. Settle, whose authoritative
knowledge and stimulating conversation contributed
so much to the making of this book.

Published by arrangement with the Estate of John Ball
and the Dominick Abel Literary Agency, Inc.

First Carroll & Graf edition 1992

Carroll & Graf Publishers, Inc.
260 Fifth Avenue
New York, NY 10001

ISBN: 0-88184-887-5

Manufactured in the United States of America

In The Heat
Of The Night

who just didn't care. Sam wove the car up the street, concentrating on missing the holes in the road. Then he looked up and saw, half a block ahead of him, a yellow distorted rectangle of light framing a window of what would be the Purdy house.

A light at this hour could mean a bellyache, or it could mean a lot of other things. Sam despised the kind of man who would peer in windows at night, but to a police officer on duty it was a different matter. He slipped the car over toward the curb so as not to disturb anyone unnecessarily and slowed up enough to check carefully why the light was burning in the Purdy kitchen at three-fifteen in the morning, though he thought he knew.

The kitchen was lighted by a single unshaded hundred-watt bulb hanging by its cord from the center of the ceiling. The thin, weary lace curtains which stretched, dead and motionless, across the open window did nothing to screen the view of the bright interior. There, plainly in view, her back turned, was Delores Purdy. As on the two previous times this had happened during the past few weeks, she wore no nightgown.

Exactly as the patrol car reached a point opposite the window, Delores lifted a small pan off the stove, turned around, and poured the pan's contents into a teacup. Sam had a full view of her sixteen-year-old breasts and the agreeable curve of her youthful thighs. Something about Delores, however, repelled him, and not even the sight of her naked body held any great interest. The reason, he guessed, was that she was always unwashed, or seemed to be. When Sam saw her raise the cup to her lips he knew that no one was ill and turned his eyes away. For a moment he contemplated warning her that she was on public view, but he decided against it because a knock at that hour might

3

wake the whole houseful of kids. And what was more, she couldn't very well answer the door with no clothes on. Sam turned at the next corner and headed back toward the highway.

Despite the lack of any visible traffic, Sam made a full stop at the intersection and then turned north. He let the car gain speed until the hot air that was forced in the open windows created the illusion of a breeze. Then for three minutes he held the pace until the city limits were in view. He lifted his foot off the gas, crossed the boundary line, and swung the car easily into the parking area of the all-night drive-in. He climbed out smoothly for a man of his size and pushed his way into the restaurant.

It was hotter inside than out. The center of the room was filled by a U-shaped counter covered with worn Formica. Down one side a row of hard plywood booths promised no comfort and little privacy. In one window a totally inadequate air-conditioner pounded out a thin stream of cool air that vanished unfelt inches from the vent where it was born. The wood walls had been painted an off white at one time; the paint had yellowed with age. Above the grill the black stain of hot grease vapor made a permanent monument to thousands of short orders that had been cooked, eaten, and forgotten.

The night counterman was a thin nineteen-year-old whose too long arms thrust below the cuffs of his soiled shirt as though they had been stretched by some infernal machine. His sharp, bony face still showed the signs of acne, his lower lip hung slightly open as though he were either accustomed to thrusting it out at people as a gesture of defiance or didn't know how to make up his mind. At the moment Sam entered, he was jack-knifed across the counter, resting his weight on his elbows, and appeared completely occupied by the vi-

4

olent comic book he had open before him.

In the presence of the law, he quickly slid his reading matter under the counter, squared his narrow shoulders, and prepared himself for the coming minutes he would spend with the guardian of the sleeping city. He reached for a thick coffee mug as Sam sank onto one of the three remaining counter stools whose upholstered tops were still intact.

"No coffee, Ralph, it's too hot," Sam said. "Give me a king Coke instead." He took off his uniform cap and drew his right arm across his forehead.

The night man scooped a scratched glass half full of shaved ice, uncapped a bottle, and filled the glass up with liquid and foam.

When the drink had settled down, Sam emptied the glass, chewed a sliver of ice into liquid, and then asked, "Who won the fight tonight?"

"Ricci," the counterman answered immediately. "Split decision. But he still gets a shot at the title."

Sam refilled his glass and drained it once more before he offered an opinion. "Good thing Ricci won. I don't go much for the Italians, but at least a white man gets a chance at the title."

The counterman nodded in quick approval. "We got six black champs now, all the top divisions. I don't see how they can fight that good." He pressed his hands against the counter and spread his bony fingers in a futile attempt to make them look strong and powerful. He looked at the thick hands of the policeman and wondered if he would ever have hands like that.

Sam helped himself to an orphan piece of cake that leaned under a clouded plastic cover on the counter. "They don't feel it when they get hit the way you or I would," he explained. "They haven't got the same nervous system. They're like animals; you've got to hit 'em with a poleax to knock 'em down, that's all. That's

5

how they win fights, why they're not afraid to get in the ring."

Ralph bobbed his head; his eyes said that Sam had pronounced the last word on the subject. He straightened the cake cover. "Mantoli was in town tonight. Brought his daughter with him. A real looker, I hear."

"I thought he wasn't due until after the first."

The counterman leaned forward, rubbing the counter with a grayed and soggy rag. "It cost more than they figured it would to finish up the bowl. Now they figure if they're going to repay the grant in time, they're going to have to charge more for the tickets. I hear Mantoli came to town to help them figure out how much people would be willing to pay."

Sam poured the last of the bottle of Coke into his glass. "I don't know," he commented. "This thing may go over all right, or it may turn out the flop of the century. I don't know anything about classical music, but I can't see crowds of people flocking here just to hear Mantoli lead a band. I know it's a symphony orchestra and all that, but the people who like that sort of thing can hear the same orchestra all winter long without having to come down here and sit on hard seats to do it. And what if it rains." He gulped the glass empty and glanced at his watch.

"Yeah. What about that. I don't care about music neither, at least not that long-hair kind," Ralph agreed, "but I say if it can put us on the map like they say it can, and bring in tourists with money to spend, maybe they'll get this joint fixed up and we'll all live a little higher on the hog."

Sam got up. "How much?" he asked.

"Fifteen cents, the cake's on the house, it was the last piece. Have a nice night, Mr. Wood."

Sam laid down a quarter and turned away. Once the counterman had dared to call him Sam. He had given a cold stare of disapproval and it had done the job. It was "Mr. Wood" now, and that was the way Sam wanted it. He climbed back into his car and reported briefly by radio before starting down the highway back into town. He settled in his seat, ready for the monotony that would make up the last part of the night.

The air was thick again as the car gained speed. For the first time since he had come on duty, Sam allowed himself to damn the pressing heat that promised a scorching day to follow. And that meant another hot night tomorrow, and perhaps another one after that. Sam slowed the car as the central area loomed ahead. The night was still deserted, but Sam drove slowly through the small downtown district as a matter of habit. He thought again of Delores Purdy. She would get married pretty young, he decided, and somebody would have plenty of fun rolling in the hay with her. It was then, a full block ahead, that he saw something lying in the road.

Sam touched the gas pedal and the car spurted ahead. In the path of the four headlamps the object grew larger until Sam braked the car to a stop in the middle of a street a few feet in front of what he could now see was a man sprawled on the pavement.

He snapped the red warning lights on and swung quickly out of the car. Before he bent over the man, he first looked quickly about him, his hand on his holstered .38, ready for instant action. He saw nothing but the silent buildings and the hard pavement stretching out in both directions. Satisfied momentarily, Sam dropped down on one knee beside the man in the street.

He was lying on his stomach, his arms above his head, his legs sprawled apart, and his face turned to the left so that his right cheek was pressed against the heavily worn concrete. He had abnormally long hair, which covered the back of his neck and then curled where it brushed the collar of his coat. Beside him, five or six feet away, a silver-handled walking stick looked strangely helpless on the hard roadway.

Sam slipped his left hand under the fallen man and tried to feel for a heartbeat. Despite the sweltering heat, the man was wearing a vest tightly buttoned; through it Sam could detect no evidence that the man was alive. Then he remembered what he had read about apparently dead bodies. Sam had not had any special course of training for his job; he had simply been put on the payroll, had been briefed for a day on his new duties, and then had gone to work. But as instructed, he had studied civic, county, and state codes and had read the two or three textbooks made available at the small headquarters building. Sam had a good memory and the information he had absorbed came back to him now in the moment of need.

Never assume that a person is dead until he has been so pronounced by a physician. He may have fainted, been stunned, or be unconscious for any of several other reasons. Persons suffering from insulin shock have often been mistaken for dead and in some cases have revived after having been taken to morgues. Unless a body has been so mutilated as to make survival impossible, such as decapitation, always assume that the person is living unless decomposition has taken place to the point where life could not possibly exist.

Sam moved quickly back to his car and picked up the radio microphone. At this hour he did not bother to use official language, but spoke quickly and clearly as soon as his call had been acknowledged.

"At the corner of Piney and the highway, approximately, man in the road, appears to be dead. No evidence of anyone else nearby, no traffic for several minutes. Send the doctor and the ambulance right away."

As he paused, Sam wondered for an instant if he had used the proper language in reporting in. This was something new to him and he wanted to handle it properly. Then the voice of the night operator snapped him out of it. "Stand by. Any identification of the victim?"

Sam thought quickly. "No, not yet," he replied. "I never saw this man before to my knowledge. However, I think I know who he is. He has long hair, wears a vest, carries a cane. A small man, not over five feet five."

"That's Mantoli," the operator exclaimed. "The conductor. The man in charge of the festival. If that's him, and if he's dead, this could be one awful mess. Repeat, stand by."

Sam pressed the mike onto its clip and walked quickly back to the fallen man. It was only nine blocks to the hospital and the ambulance would be on the scene within five minutes. As Sam bent over the man once more, he remembered the rundown dog, but this was infinitely worse.

Sam reached out his hand and laid it very gently on the back of the man's head, as though by his touch he could comfort him and tell him that help was coming quickly, that he would only have to lie on the harsh pavement for two or three minutes more, and that in the meantime he was not alone. It was while these thoughts were running through his mind that Sam became aware that something thick and sticky was oozing against his fingers. With a quick involuntary motion he jerked his hand away. The pity he had felt evaporated and a growing red anger surged up in its place.

9

— 2 —

At four minutes after four in the morning, the phone rang at the bedside of Bill Gillespie, chief of police of the city of Wells. Gillespie took a few seconds to shake himself partially awake before he answered. As he reached for the instrument he already knew that it was trouble, and probably big trouble, otherwise the night desk man would have handled it. The night man was on the line.

"Chief, I hate to wake you, but if Sam Wood is right, we may have a first-class murder on our hands."

Gillespie forced himself to sit up and swing his legs over the side of the bed. "Tourist?"

"No, not exactly. Sam has tentatively identified the body as that of Enrico Mantoli—you know, the fellow who was going to set up a music festival here. Understand, Chief, that we aren't even sure yet that the man is dead, but if he is, and if Sam's identification is correct, then somebody has knocked off our local celebrity and our whole music-festival deal probably has gone to pot."

Bill Gillespie was fully awake now. While he felt automatically for his slippers with his feet, he knew that he was expected to take command. The schooling in his profession he had back in Texas told him what to say. "All right, listen to me. I'll come right down. Get a doctor and the ambulance there right away, a photographer, and dig up a couple more men. Have Wood stay where he is until I get there. You know the routine?"

The night desk man, who never before had had to deal with a murder, answered that he did. As soon as he hung up, Gillespie rose to his full six feet four and began quickly to climb into his clothes, running over in his mind exactly what he would do when he reached the murder scene. He had been chief of police and a Wells resident for only nine weeks, and now he would have to prove himself. As he bent to tie his shoes, he knew that he could trust himself to do the right thing, but he still wished that the hurdles immediately before him had already been cleared.

Despite the fact that he was only thirty-two, Bill Gillespie had abundant confidence in his own ability to meet whatever challenges were thrown at him. His size made it possible for him to look down literally on most men. His forcefulness, which had cost him the girl he had wanted to marry, swept away many normal obstacles as though they had never existed. If he had a murder on his hands he would solve it, and no one would dare to question him while he was in the process.

Then he remembered that he had not been told where the murder was. He picked up the phone angrily and misdialed in his haste. He slammed the instrument back into its cradle before what he knew would be a wrong number could ring, and then, forcing himself to be calm, tried again.

The night police desk man, who had been expecting the call, answered immediately. "Where is it?" Gillespie demanded.

"On the highway, Chief, just below Piney. The ambulance is there and the doctor has pronounced the victim dead. No positive identification yet."

11

"All right," the chief acknowledged, and dropped the instrument into position. He didn't like having to admit that he had had to call back to know where to go. He should have been told the body's position the first time.

Bill Gillespie's personal car was equipped with a siren, red lights in the rear window, and a police radio set. He jumped in, kicked the starter, and jerked the car away from the curb and up to speed without any regard whatever for the cold engine. In less than five minutes he saw ahead of him the police car, the ambulance, and a little knot of people gathered in the middle of the highway. Gillespie drove up quickly, set the brake, and was out of the car before it had come to a complete stop.

Without speaking to anyone, he strode rapidly to where the body still lay in the street, then squatted down and began to run his hands quickly over the fallen man. "Where's his wallet?" he demanded.

Sam Wood stepped forward to reply. "It's missing. At least I didn't find it on the body."

"Any positive identification?" Gillespie snapped.

The young doctor who had come with the ambulance answered that. "It's Enrico Mantoli, the conductor. He was the spark plug behind the musical festival we've been planning here."

"I know that," Gillespie retorted curtly, and turned his attention again to the body. He had a strong desire to tell it to sit up, wipe the dirt off its face, and tell him what happened, who did it. But this was one man whom he could not command. All right then, it would have to be done some other way. Gillespie looked up.

"Sam, take your car, check the railroad station and the north end of town to see if anyone is crazy enough to try to hitchhike out of here. Wait a minute." He turned his head quickly toward the doctor. "How long has this man been dead?"

"Less than an hour, I should say possibly less than forty-five minutes. Whoever did it can't be too far away."

Gillespie allowed an expression of angry annoyance to cross his face. "All I asked you was how long he has been dead; you don't have to tell me my job, I'll tell you. I want photographs of the body from all angles, including some shots long enough to show its position relative to the curb and the buildings on the west side of the street. Then mark the position in chalk outline and barricade the area to keep traffic off this spot. After that you can take the body away." He stood up and saw Sam standing quietly by. "What did I tell you to do?" he demanded.

"You told me to wait a minute," Sam answered evenly.

"All right then, you can get going. Hop to it."

Sam moved quickly to his patrol car and drove away with enough speed to avoid any possible criticism later. As he headed toward the railroad station, for a brief moment he allowed himself to hope that Gillespie would somehow make a public fool of himself and bungle the case. Then he realized that such a thought was totally unworthy of a sworn peace officer and he resolved that no matter what happened, his part would be done promptly and well.

At the last moment, as he approached the silent railroad station, he slowed his car down to avoid giving any undue warning to a possible murderer lurking inside. Sam pulled up close to the wooden platform and climbed out without hesitation. The station was a small one which dated back at least fifty years; at night it was inadequately lighted by a few dusty bulbs which seemed as ageless as the worn hard benches or the unyielding tile floor. As Sam walked rapidly toward the main waiting-room door, he had a sudden desire to loosen the pressure of his uniform cap. He rejected the idea at once and entered the station every inch a police officer, his right hand on his gun. The waiting room was deserted.

Sam sniffed the air rapidly and detected nothing to suggest that anyone had been there recently. No fresh cigarette smoke, only the habitual aroma of all such railroad stations, the evidence of thousands of nameless people who had passed through and gone on.

The ticket window was closed; the glass panel was down. Posted inside was a square of cardboard with the arrival times of the night trains printed in heavy crayon. Sam looked carefully about the room once more while he thought. If the murderer was here, he probably did not have a gun. He had killed by hitting the dead man on the back of the head with a blunt instrument, and with a blunt instrument Sam was confident he could deal. He bent and checked the small area under the benches. It was clear except for dirt and a few bits of paper.

Striding through the room, Sam pushed open the door to the train platform and looked both ways. The platform, too, was deserted. Walking with firm, authoritative steps, Sam passed the locked baggage-room door, which he tested and found secure, and paused by the dingier door over which a white board sign specified COLORED. With his right hand once more on his sidearm, Sam pushed into the poorly lighted room and then drew a quick gulp of breath. There was someone there.

Sam sized him up at a glance, and knew at once that he did not belong in Wells. He was fairly slender and dressed up in city clothes, including a white shirt and a tie. Sam guessed that he might be about thirty, but

14

it was always hard to tell about blacks. Instead of being stretched out on the bench, he was wide awake and sitting up straight as though he were expecting something to happen. His coat was off and laid neatly beside him. He had been reading a paperback book up to the moment Sam entered; when he looked up, Sam saw that his face lacked the broad nose and thick, heavy lips that characterized so many southern laborers. His nose was almost like a white man's and the line of his mouth was straight and disciplined. If he had been a little lighter, Sam would have seen white blood in him, but his skin was too black for that.

The Negro forgot his book and let his hands fall into his lap while he looked up into Sam's broad face.

Sam took immediate command. "On your feet, black boy," he ordered, and crossed the room in five quick steps.

The Negro reached for his coat. "No you don't!" Sam knocked his arm aside and with a single swift motion spun his man around and clamped his own powerful forearm hard under the Negro's chin. In this position Sam could control him easily and still leave his right hand and arm free. Swiftly Sam searched his captive, an action which the Negro appeared too frightened to resist. When he had finished, Sam released the pressure on the man's windpipe and issued further orders. "Stand against the wall, face to it. Put your hands up, fingers apart, and lean against them. Keep them up where I can see them. Don't move until I tell you to."

The Negro obeyed without a word. When his order had been executed, Sam picked up the Negro's coat and felt inside the breast pocket. There was a wallet and it felt unusually thick.

With a strange prickle of excitement Sam pulled the wallet out and checked its contents. It was well stuffed with money. Sam ran his thumb down the edges of the

15

bills; they were mostly tens and twenties; when he stopped his riffling at the long, narrow oval that marked a fifty, Sam was satisfied. He snapped the wallet shut and put it into his own pocket. The prisoner remained motionless, his feet out from the wall, leaning forward with part of his weight supported by his outstretched hands. Sam looked at him carefully again from the rear. He guessed that the suspect was around a hundred and fifty pounds, maybe a little more, but not much. He was about five feet nine, large enough to have done the job. There was a hint of a crease on the back of his trousers, so his suit had at some time been pressed. He did not have the big butt Sam was accustomed to on many Negroes, but that didn't mean he was frail. When Sam slapped him to see if he had a weapon, the Negro's body was firm and hard under his hand.

Sam folded the man's coat across his own arm. "Go out the door to your left," he ordered. "There's a police car in the drive. Get in the back seat and shut the door. Make one false move and I'll drop you right then with a bullet in your spine. Now move."

The Negro turned as directed, walked out onto the city side of the platform, and obediently climbed into the back seat of Sam's waiting car. The prisoner slammed the door just enough to be sure that it was properly latched and settled back in the seat. He made no move to do anything other than what he was directed.

Sam climbed in behind the wheel. There were no inside door handles in the patrol car and he knew that his prisoner could not escape. For a moment he thought of the way Mantoli had been killed—hit over the head presumably from the rear and probably by the prime suspect who was sitting behind him at that moment. Then Sam reassured himself with the thought that there was nothing in the rear seat which the Negro could use for a weapon, and with a bare-hand attack Sam could easily deal. He would have welcomed one; the prospect of a little action was attractive, particularly with someone as easy to handle as his captive.

Sam picked up the radio microphone and spoke tersely. "Wood from the railroad station. Bringing in a colored suspect." He paused, thought a moment, and decided to add nothing else. The rest of it could wait until he got to the station. The less police business put on the air the better.

The prisoner made no sound as Sam drove, smoothly and expertly, the eleven blocks to the police station. Two men were waiting at the drive-in entrance when he got there; Sam waved them aside, confident of his ability to handle his prisoner without help. He took his time as he climbed out, walked around the car, and swung the rear door open. "Out," he ordered.

The Negro climbed out and submitted without protest when Sam seized his upper arm and piloted him into the police station. Sam walked in properly, exactly as the illustrations in the manuals he had studied told him to do. With his powerful left arm he controlled his prisoner, his right hand resting, instantly ready, on his police automatic. Sam regretted that there was no one to take a picture of that moment, and then realized that once more he had forgotten himself and the dignity of his position.

As Sam turned the corner toward the row of cells, he was intercepted by the night desk man, who pointed silently to the office of Chief Gillespie. Sam nodded, steered his man up to the door, and knocked.

"Come in." Gillespie's strident voice echoed through the door. Sam turned the knob with his right hand, pushed his man through the opening, and waited before Gillespie's desk. The chief was pretending that he was occupied with some papers before him. Then he laid down the pen he had been holding and stared hard at the prisoner for a full twenty seconds. Sam could not see the prisoner's reaction and did not dare to turn his head to look for fear of breaking the psychological spell.

"What's your name!" Gillespie demanded suddenly. The question came out of his lips like a shot.

The Negro astonished Sam by speaking, for the first time, in a calm, unhurried voice. "My name is Tibbs, Virgil Tibbs," he replied, and then stood completely still. Sam relaxed his hold on the man's arm, but the prisoner made no attempt to sit in the empty chair beside him.

"What were you doing in the station?" This time the question was slightly less explosive, more matter-of-fact.

The Negro answered without shifting his weight. "I was waiting for the five-seventeen train for Washington." The scene of complete silence was repeated: Sam did not move, Gillespie sat perfectly still, and the prisoner made no attempt to do anything.

"When and how did you get into town?" This time Gillespie's question was deceptively mild and patient in tone.

"I came in on the twelve-thirty-five. It was three-quarters of an hour late."

"*What* twelve-thirty-five?" Gillespie barked suddenly.

The prisoner's tone in answering was unchanged. "The one from downstate. The local." The idea forced itself on Sam that this was an educated black, one of the sort that hung around the United Nations in New York, according to the newsreels. That might make it a little harder for Gillespie. Sam clamped his teeth together and held the corners of his mouth firm so he could not betray himself by smiling.

18

"What were you doing downstate?"

"I went to visit my mother."

There was a pause before the next question. Sam guessed that it would be an important one and that Gillespie was waiting deliberately to give it added force.

"Where did you get the money for your train fare?"

Before the prisoner could answer, Sam came to life. He fished the Negro's wallet from his own pocket and handed it to Gillespie. The chief looked quickly in the money compartment and slammed the wallet down hard onto the top of his desk. "Where did you get all *this* dough?" he demanded, and rose just enough from the seat of his chair so that the prisoner could see his size.

"I earned it," the Negro replied.

Gillespie dropped back into his chair, satisfied. Colored couldn't make money like that, or keep it if they did, and he knew it. The verdict was in, and the load was off his shoulders.

"Where do you work?" he demanded in a voice that told Sam the chief was ready to go home and back to bed.

"In Pasadena, California."

Bill Gillespie permitted himself a grim smile. Two thousand miles was a long way to most people, especially to colored. Far enough to make them think that a checkup wouldn't be made. Bill leaned forward across his desk to drive the next question home.

"And what do you do in Pasadena, California, that makes you money like that?"

The prisoner took the barest moment before he replied.

"I'm a police officer," he said.

— 3 —

As a matter of principle Sam Wood did not like Negroes, at least not on anything that approached a man-to-man basis. It therefore confused him for a moment when he discovered within himself a stab of admiration for the slender man who stood beside him. Sam was a sportsman and therefore he enjoyed seeing someone, anyone, stand up successfully to Wells's new chief of police.

Until Gillespie arrived in town, Sam Wood had been rated a big man, but Gillespie's towering size automatically demoted Sam Wood to near normal stature. The new chief was only three years his senior—too young, Sam thought, for his job, even in a city as small as Wells. Furthermore, Gillespie came from Texas, a state for which Sam felt no fraternal affection. But most of all Sam resented, consciously, Gillespie's hard, inconsiderate, and demanding manner. Sam arrived at the conclusion that he felt no liking for the Negro, only rich satisfaction in seeing Gillespie apparently confounded. Before he could think any further, Gillespie was looking at him.

"Did you question this man at all before you brought him in?" Gillespie demanded.

"No, sir," Sam answered. The "sir" stuck in his throat.

"Why not?" Gillespie barked the question in what Sam decided was a deliberately offensive manner. But if the Negro could keep his composure, Sam decided, he could, too. He thought for an instant and then replied as calmly as he could.

"Your orders were to check the railroad station and then to look for possible hitchhikers or anyone else worth checking. When I found this ni—this man in the railroad station, I brought him in immediately, so I could carry out the rest of your orders. Shall I go now?"

Sam was proud of himself. He knew he wasn't much with words, but that, he felt sure, had been a good speech.

"I want to finish checking this man out first." Gillespie looked toward Tibbs. "You say you're a cop in California?"

"Yes, I am," Tibbs replied, still standing patiently beside the empty hard chair.

"Prove it."

"There's an ID card in my wallet."

Gillespie picked up the wallet from his desk with the air of handling something distasteful and somewhat unclean. He opened the pass-card section and stared hard at the small white card in the first transparent sleeve, then snapped the wallet shut and tossed it carelessly toward the young Negro. Tibbs caught it and slipped it quietly into his pocket.

"What have you been doing all night?" There was an edge of irritation in Gillespie's voice now. The voice was trying to pick a fight, and daring anyone to defy it.

"After I got off the train, I went in the station and waited. I didn't leave the station platform." There was still no change in Tibb's manner, something which Gillespie apparently found irritating. He changed the topic abruptly.

"You know we wouldn't let the likes of you try to be a cop down here, don't you?"

He waited; the room remained still.

"You knew enough to stay out of the white waiting room. You knew that, didn't you?" Once more Gillespie pressed his huge hands against the desk and positioned himself as if to rise.

"Yes, I knew that."

Gillespie made a decision. "All right, you stick around awhile. I'm going to check up on you. Take care of him, Sam."

Without speaking, Sam Wood turned around and followed Virgil Tibbs out of the room. Ordinarily he would not have permitted a Negro to precede him through a doorway, but this Negro did not wait for him to go first and Sam decided it was a bad moment to raise an issue. As soon as the two men had left, Gillespie raised one massive fist and slammed it down hard on the top of his desk. Then he scooped up the phone and dictated a wire to the police department of Pasadena, California.

Sam Wood showed Virgil Tibbs to a hard bench in the small detention room. Tibbs thanked him, sat down, pulled out the paperback book that he had had in the station, and returned to reading. Sam glanced at the cover. It was *On Understanding Science* by Conant. Sam sat down and wished that he, too, had a book to read.

When the sky began to gray through the window, and then grew streaked with curiously dirty stripes of high clouds against a lightening background, Sam knew that he would not be driving his patrol car anymore that night—it was too late for that. He began to ache from sitting on the hard bench. He wanted a cup of coffee despite the heat; he wanted to move around. He was debating whether he wanted to stand up and stretch, and make a slight exhibit of himself doing so, when Gillespie abruptly appeared in the doorway.

Tibbs looked up with quiet inquiry in his eyes.

"You can go if you want to," Gillespie said, looking at Tibbs. "You've missed your train and there won't be another one until afternoon. If you want to wait here, we'll see you get some breakfast."

"Thank you," Tibbs acknowledged. Sam decided this was his cue, and stood up. As soon as Gillespie cleared the doorway, Sam walked out and down the short hall to the door marked MEN—WHITE. The night desk man was inside, washing his hands. Something about the twist of the man's mouth told Sam there was undisclosed news. "Got anything, Pete?" he asked.

Pete nodded, splashed water over his face, and buried it in a towel. When he came up for air, he replied. "Chief got a wire a few minutes ago." He paused, bent down, and checked that all the toilet compartments were empty. "From Pasadena. Gillespie sent one out that said: 'We have serious homicide here. Request information re Virgil Tibbs, colored, who claims to be member Pasadena Police Department. Holding him as possible suspect.'"

"I don't blame him for checking up," Sam said.

"Wait till you hear what he got back." Pete lowered his voice so that Sam had to take a step closer to hear him. "'Confirm Virgil Tibbs member Pasadena Police Department past ten years. Present rank investigator. Specialist homicide, other major crimes. Reputation excellent. Advise if his services needed your area. Agree homicide serious.'"

"Wow," Sam said softly.

"Exactly," Pete agreed. "I bet Gillespie doesn't know a damn thing about homicide investigation. If he doesn't clear this one up, and fast, the whole town will be down on his neck. So he has the offer of a specialist who is both chief suspect and a nig—" He paused when Sam shot up his hand as a warning. Footsteps passed down the corridor and disappeared into silence.

"What I want to know," Sam inquired, "is if Gillespie is as stupid as I think he is, how did he get this job in the first place? He was supposed to have been a hotshot in Texas, wasn't he?"

Pete shook his head. "He was never a cop; he's over the height limit. He was a jailor—a strong-arm boy who could handle the drunks. After three years of that, he answered an ad and got this job. He probably figures it will set him up for something bigger after a little while. But if he flubs this one he's done for, and he knows it."

"How did you get all this dope?"

Pete pressed his lips together and grinned. "I've been in this business a long time, and I've made quite a few friends here and there. I think I'll stick around awhile and see what happens. I go on days beginning tomorrow so it will look all right. How about you?"

"I think I will, too," Sam agreed.

Ten minutes later, the body of Maestro Enrico Mantoli was brought in. The hospital had refused to hold it any longer. When Pete went to Gillespie's office to notify his chief of that fact in person, he found him with his hands thrust inside the waistband of his trousers and his mind obviously miles away. Pete waited until he was recognized, conveyed the news, and retreated rapidly while he was still in good order. A few moments later, Gillespie came out of his office, stalked down the corridor, and paused before the door of the detention room. He stared at Tibbs, who sat there reading. When he saw Gillespie, he looked up and waited for the big man to speak.

"Pasadena tells me you're supposed to be a homicide investigator," Gillespie barked.

"I've done that," Tibbs replied.

"Ever look at dead bodies?" Gillespie put a leer into the question.

"Oftener than I like."

"I'm going over to look at one now. Suppose you come along."

Tibbs got to his feet. "After you, sir," he said.

No one in the small morgue looked especially surprised when Virgil Tibbs came in silently in the wake of the towering Gillespie. The police morgue was a modest facility with a single surgical table in the middle of the room, and a half-dozen grim drawers like a massive filing cabinet in one wall. There was a wood desk and a chair at one side and next to it a cabinet half filled with instruments. The chief walked without hesitation to the slab in the middle of the room, bent over and stared hard at the dead man. He walked around him twice. Once he reached out and carefully bent the dead man's arm at the elbow, then he replaced it as it had been. Finally he squatted down and scrutinized the top of the man's head where he had been struck. Then he rose once more to his feet. With a long arm and an almost accusing finger, he pointed. "Virgil here works for the Pasadena Police Department investigating homicides. He wants to look at the body. Let him."

Having made his pronouncement, Gillespie stalked out to the men's room to wash.

As soon as he had removed both dirt and the feel of the dead man from his hands, Bill Gillespie began to think of breakfast. He had given up completely any idea of trying to complete his night's sleep. He decided also that there was no need to return home and shave; good grooming was not expected under emergency conditions and the fact that he showed visible signs of his extra duty might well be to his advantage. He decided to go and eat.

He walked out through the station, folded himself behind the wheel of his car, and U-turned fast enough to skid at the finish. Six minutes later, he slid the car to a stop at the all-night drive-in, terrifying the youthful attendant simply by the way he planted himself on a counter stool. "I want the ranch breakfast," he ordered.

The night man nodded quickly and set to work at once to prepare the wheat cakes, eggs, bacon, potatoes, toast, and coffee that made up the ranch package. Striving to please, he broke the yolks of both eggs, scraped them away, and tried two more. This time he succeeded. By the time all the food was served, he had refilled Gillespie's coffee cup three times. When at last the big man had finished eating, paid without leaving a tip, and left, the boy's hand was shaking so hard he had difficulty drawing a glass of water to slake his own thirst. Apart from stating his order, Gillespie had not said a single word, but the furrows on his brow had betrayed the fact that he had been concentrating on some thought or idea which he did not like.

On the way back to the station, Gillespie drove more slowly. The sun was up now and there was traffic on the highway. Part of his caution was dictated by the fact that he did not want to be detected flouting the traffic laws he was sworn to enforce, the rest by the fact that he wanted time to think.

How, he asked himself, do you go about catching a murderer? Normally you would probably start checking up to see who held a grudge against the deceased, but this was a simple case of robbery. He had learned two things during his brief visit to the morgue—that the dead man's wallet was missing and that he had been reputed to carry considerable sums on his person. All right then, how do you find the man who hit the deceased over the head in the dead of night and got away without a single witness being anywhere around?

How do you find the man who wants more money than he is entitled to, how do you trace money without serial numbers, without anything to go on other than the fact that it exists? There won't be footprints to pick up in plaster in the middle of a paved highway, or any usable tire marks. Just what the hell do you do?

Well, you might ask to borrow a homicide expert. And then what do you do if you have one dropped into your lap and he has a black skin?

Gillespie changed his mind and drove home. He shaved, put some deodorant under his armpits in lieu of a shower, rebrushed his hair, and drove back through the morning traffic to the police station. On the way he made one decision: he would get rid of Tibbs as soon as possible. The Pasadena boys had been pulling his leg when they recommended him. Nobody could tell him that a colored man could do anything he couldn't do.

Reinforced by this thought, Gillespie climbed the steps to the station three at a time, stopped at the desk, and demanded, "Where's Tibbs?"

The day man, who clearly knew fully what was going on, said, "I believe, sir, he's still examining the body."

"Still examining the body!" Gillespie exploded. "What the hell is he trying to do, find out how a man died who was hit over the head hard enough to break his skull?"

"I looked in a minute before I came on duty," the day man replied. "At that time he was removing the dirt from under the fingernails. He asked if we had a microscope and I said that we didn't. Then he took a ring off the corpse's finger and looked at the initials inside. By that time I had to leave to come on duty."

When Gillespie reached his office, he found Sam Wood waiting for him. "I thought I had better report to you before I went home," Sam explained, "in case you wanted to ask me any questions or have me stay on duty for a while."

Gillespie allowed himself to look human for a moment. "That was very thoughtful of you, Wood," he acknowledged. "Sit down and tell me what you think of our colored friend, *Officer* Virgil Tibbs."

Sam sat down. "I think he's got guts," he answered, looking at his chief. Then he changed his tone, as though the statement, in retrospect, had been too strong for him. "At least, he isn't afraid to handle a corpse."

"I thought he said he didn't like to examine bodies," Gillespie interjected.

"I took that to mean that he didn't like homicides," Sam replied.

"I thought homicides were supposed to be his business."

The conversation was interrupted when Virgil Tibbs appeared in the doorway.

"Excuse me, gentlemen," he said, "but could you tell me where I can wash?"

Gillespie answered immediately. "The colored washroom is down the hall to your right."

Tibbs nodded and disappeared.

"There's no soap or towels down there," Sam reminded Gillespie.

"That's what he's got a shirttail for," Gillespie snapped back.

Sam recrossed his legs the other way, tightened for a moment, and then relaxed. It was none of his affair. He wanted to leave, but when he half started to rise, he remembered that he had offered to stay on duty and that he had not received an answer. He looked at Gillespie, who, in turn, was staring down at his immense hands, which he had folded on top of his desk. The storm clouds began to gather in his face. Then he looked up. "Suppose you take your car and see if you can locate

Mantoli's daughter. I heard she was a house guest of the Endicotts. Break the news to her and get her down here to make a positive identification of the body. I know that it will be difficult, but that is part of our job. You had better leave right away if you want to get to her before she hears it some other way. We haven't given anything out, but you can't keep a secret in this town very long."

Virgil Tibbs reappeared in the open doorway and looked at Gillespie. "Do you wish the results of my examination, sir?" he asked.

Gillespie leaned back at a slight angle; because of his size, it was as far as he could go without risking a fall backward. "I've thought about it, Virgil, and I've decided that the best thing would be for you to leave town on the next train. This is no place for you. I know all I need to know about the body. Tell your boss when you get home that I appreciate his offer of your services, but they are quite unacceptable and you know why."

Gillespie leaned forward again. "Oh, yes," he added. "I'm having a release typed up absolving us from false arrest charges in your case. I want you to sign it before you go."

"As one policeman to another," Tibbs said evenly, "I don't intend to sue you or Mr. Wood for false arrest. You don't need to bother with a release. Thanks for your hospitality."

An arm suddenly pushed Tibbs aside and Pete, his face flushed, appeared in the doorway. "We've got him, Chief, dead to rights. It's Harvey Oberst. He's been in trouble before. The boys picked him up and found Mantoli's wallet on him."

Gillespie looked back at Tibbs, who was still visible on one side of the doorway. "Like I said, Virgil, we know our business down here. Go home."

— 4 —

Bill Gillespie looked at Sam Wood. "You had anything to eat?" he asked.

"Not this morning," Sam replied.

"Then stay here and get some chow. Let Arnold go and pick up the Mantoli girl."

"No, that's all right, I'll go. I know how to get to the Endicott place, and I don't think Arnold does. Speaking of eating, we do owe Virgil some breakfast—we promised it to him."

"I told him to beat it."

Sam Wood sensed that he could go a little further. "Yes, sir, but there is no train for hours and the only bus through here going north doesn't carry colored. It's my fault he missed his train. Since he *is* a cop, maybe we ought to let him wait here"—Sam paused as inspiration hit him—"so he'll at least speak well of us when he gets back to Pasadena."

Gillespie recognized diplomacy as a necessary evil. "All right. But there're no colored restaurants around here. Get hold of Virgil before he leaves, send him back in here, and have Pete bring him in a bologna sandwich or whatever he can pick up. It might be a good idea to let him see us wrap this one up—show him that we know how to handle men down here."

His point won, Sam nodded, and retreated rapidly before Gillespie could change his mind again. He found

30

Tibbs saying his good-byes to Pete in the lobby. "Virgil," Sam reported, "the chief just remembered that he had promised you some breakfast. He wants you to go back to his office." Sam struggled with himself for a moment and was glad when right triumphed. "And thanks for letting me off the hook on false arrest. You could have made it tough."

Virgil Tibbs started to hold out his hand and then, to Sam's immense relief, shifted his coat to his other arm instead. "Don't mention it, Mr. Wood. I know you would extend me the same courtesy in Pasadena."

For a moment Sam was ashamed of the fact that if Tibbs *had* held out his hand, he would have had to look away. What with Pete there and all that. But Tibbs had saved him the embarrassment, and for that he was grateful. He left to carry out his unpleasant errand.

Tibbs walked back down the corridor to Gillespie's office. "Mr. Wood said you wanted to see me," he said.

Gillespie waved him to a chair against the wall. "I've sent for some breakfast for you. You can wait here until it comes; the boys are pretty busy right now. Meanwhile we've caught our murderer."

"You have a confession?" Tibbs inquired.

"Don't need one," Gillespie retorted. "I've just read the folder on him. Nineteen years old and in trouble twice already. Once petty theft and once for playing around with a girl named Delores Purdy. He had Mantoli's wallet on him."

"It sounds like a good start," Virgil Tibbs agreed.

"You'll see how good a start it is," Gillespie declared, and reached for his intercom. "Send Oberst in here," he ordered.

While he was waiting, Gillespie flashed a look toward Tibbs. "Do you know what 'poor white trash' means down here, Virgil?" he asked.

"I've heard the term," Tibbs replied.

There were footsteps in the corridor and then a short, chunky policeman shoved a grown boy into the office. The prisoner was wearing handcuffs. He was too slender for even his moderate height. His blue denim pants fitted him so tightly that the awkward angles of his legs were outlined in sharp relief. His eyes were blinking rapidly—looking back to his hands once more. He seemed to sway on his feet, as though balancing upright was a conscious effort almost beyond his skill.

Gillespie drew himself up and roared at the prisoner. "Sit down!"

Harvey Oberst sat down simply by letting his body go limp in front of the chair. His thin buttocks hit the hard seat with a bump, but he didn't seem to care. He rested his hands in his lap and let his head fall to one side as though there was no point in trying to hold it upright any longer.

The seconds ticked on as Bill Gillespie waited for the prisoner to become fully intimidated. Oberst, however, didn't react.

Gillespie looked up at the arresting officer. "Have you got it?" he demanded.

The stocky policeman reached inside his tunic and produced a heavily tooled wallet thick with its contents. Gillespie took it, examined it in detail, and peered at the identification cards which it contained. "You can take the cuffs off him," he said almost conversationally.

As soon as he was released from the handcuffs, Harvey Oberst began to rub his wrists, first one and then the other, but he said nothing.

"Whatcha do it for?" Gillespie demanded.

Oberst drew breath and lifted his head up. "Because it was just lying there. Right where I could see it. Full of money. I looked; he was dead and couldn't use it. It was just lying there. If I hadn't a taken it, somebody else would of. I needed it bad; so I took it." He paused.

"That's all," he added apologetically.

"That is, after you killed him," Gillespie prompted.

The prisoner jumped to his feet, his face twisted so tightly that he seemed to be in sudden acute pain. "I took his wallet," he screamed. "Because he was dead I took his wallet. I needed it, bad—but I didn't kill him!" His voice cracked on the last words so that he croaked them out, robbed of any strength of meaning.

Oberst tried again. With his left forefinger he thumped himself on the chest. "I didn't kill him, I wouldn't of had to kill him even if I wanted to grab his dough. He was a real little guy, I seen him before. I could've handled him easy if I'd wanted to. *I just picked up his wallet, I tell you!*" Suddenly he gave up and dropped back into the chair. This time he let his head roll forward until his chin almost touched his chest.

Bill Gillespie waved his hand in a gesture of dismissal. "Book him," he ordered. "Suspicion of murder." He rocked back in his chair as far as he cared and stared at the ceiling. He continued to look there until the prisoner had been taken away.

When a cell door could be heard clanging shut a few moments later, Gillespie relaxed visibly and looked at Virgil Tibbs, who still sat on the uncomfortable chair at the side of the room. "Well, that clears it up," he commented.

"It helps," Tibbs agreed.

"How much more help do you want?" Gillespie asked, his voice somewhat closer to a normal level for a change.

"It eliminates the superficial motive," Tibbs replied, "it means digging a little deeper. I expected it, but it is an advantage to see it confirmed."

Gillespie swiveled to face Tibbs, an amused smile dawning on his face. "Don't tell me you bought that kid's story. I thought you were supposed to be the hotshot cop, the deadly manhunter, the Sherlock of the Pacific. If you're a cop, I'm an anteater."

Arnold appeared in the doorway carrying a waxed-paper-wrapped sandwich in one hand and a paper container of coffee in the other. Without comment he handed them to Tibbs, then turned toward his chief. "Is he our boy?" he asked.

Gillespie waved his hand toward Tibbs, who was unwrapping his sandwich. "Ask him," he suggested.

Arnold looked obediently at Tibbs. "Well?" he asked.

"He's innocent of the murder, I'm almost certain of that," Tibbs replied.

"Now tell him why," Gillespie invited.

"Because he's left-handed," Tibbs answered, and bit into his sandwich.

Arnold looked at Gillespie. "Go on," he said.

Tibbs waited a moment until his mouth was empty. "When I examined the body of the deceased this morning," Tibbs explained patiently, "it was evident that the fatal blow had been struck by a blunt instrument at an angle of about seventeen degrees from the right as the skull is viewed from the rear. That makes it almost certain that the assailant was right-handed. If you'll pick up your desk ruler for a moment by one end, Chief Gillespie, I'll explain the point."

To Arnold's utter amazement, Gillespie complied.

"Now imagine that you want to strike something with it at about the level of your own shoulders, or even a little higher. If you hold the ruler tightly, you will see that it is almost impossible to hold it straight out; your wrist isn't built that way. If you want to point it toward the right, you will have to turn your hand over, palm up, to do it. Even to hit straight ahead, you have to turn your wrist ninety degrees."

Gillespie looked at the stick in his hand and then

laid it back on top of his desk. "And you think Oberst is left-handed," he said.

"I know he is," the Negro replied. "You remember when he thumped himself in the chest when he was trying to defend himself. Even if he was ambidextrous, he would still use his primary hand to do that, and he thumped himself with his left forefinger. I noticed when he walked in that he was probably innocent, but that confirmed it, in my judgment." Tibbs took another bite from his sandwich and moistened it with a sip of the thick black coffee.

"I didn't ask if you wanted sugar," Arnold said.

"This is fine, thank you," Tibbs replied.

"You just looked at that guy and decided that he was probably innocent. What was that, intuition?" Gillespie asked.

"No, his shoes," Tibbs answered, "and the fact that he needed a shave."

Suddenly Gillespie fell silent. Arnold waited for his superior to ask why shoes and a shave were important. Then he realized that Gillespie would not do that; it would be a comedown for him and Bill Gillespie did not take kindly to comedowns. Arnold cleared his throat.

He waited until Tibbs had his mouth empty between bites and then asked, "Why?"

"Consider the circumstances of the attack," Tibbs replied. "Mantoli was hit over the head from behind. That means that he was either assaulted by someone he knew and trusted, who stepped behind him for a moment and then hit him, or, more likely, someone sneaked up on him quietly enough to hit him without warning. If Mantoli had ben warned, even by a second, he would have turned his head somewhat and the blow would have landed at a different angle on the skull."

"I can see that," Arnold agreed.

"The suspect is wearing hard leather heels," Tibbs continued, "and he has steel plates on them to make them wear longer. In those shoes every step he takes is noisy and he couldn't possibly have made a surprise attack with them on."

"A man can change his shoes any time," Gillespie interrupted.

"You're correct, of course, Chief Gillespie," Tibbs agreed, "but you mentioned to me that this man is 'poor white trash,' which suggests that he has only a limited number of pairs of shoes and doesn't change them too often. Judging by the stubble on his chin I would guess that he was up all night. If he went home to change his shoes, he would probably shave, too. He does so regularly; there were razor nicks under his chin that showed that."

"I didn't see them," Gillespie challenged.

"I'm sitting at a lower angle than you are, Chief Gillespie," Tibbs answered, "and the light was much better from my side."

"You're pretty sure of yourself, aren't you, Virgil," Gillespie retorted. "Incidentally, Virgil is a pretty fancy name for a black boy like you. What do they call you around home where you come from?"

"They call me Mr. Tibbs," Virgil answered.

Sam Wood drove slowly as he guided his patrol car up the road that led to the Endicott place. Although the sun was blazing down now, the intense heat seemed more bearable, largely because he expected the days to be hot. The thing that bothered him was the hot nights, for somehow the darkness and the setting of the sun ought to bring relief. When they didn't, the discomfort seemed twice as great.

The road climbed steadily. The main section of Wells

was now several hundred feet below and there was still a distance to go to reach the very top of the hill where the Endicotts had their home. Sam knew where it was, as did nearly everyone in Wells, since the Endicotts were known to have money, but he had never met them or been to their home. As he drove he tried to form in his mind the sentences that he would use in breaking the news. It would not be easy. Somehow he imagined that Mantoli's daughter, the Endicotts' house guest, did not have a mother. Now she would be all alone in the world—unless, of course, she had a husband. Probably she did, he decided; Italian girls married early, had too many kids, and got fat.

The road leveled off at the top of the hill, ending at a small parking lot which Sam quickly estimated would hold six or eight cars. He parked carefully and closed the door quietly as he stepped to the ground. The sun seemed brighter up here, but the air, he thought, was not quite as hot. It was a magnificent location; despite the seriousness of his errand, Sam could not help being moved by the sweeping panoramic view of the Great Smokies. Long rows of serrated mountains lifted their peaks all the way to the distant horizon. Sam walked toward the front door, which opened for him before he had an opportunity to ring.

He was received by a woman who waited, with an air of both hospitality and restraint, for him to state his business. Sam liked her immediately. She was well into her fifties, but the years which she had lived had treated her with great respect. In a quiet, tasteful linen dress, her body was molded into the same contours that had been attractive thirty years before. Her face was unwrinkled, her hair was beautifully cut and shaped. She waited while Sam took the last steps to reach the doorstep.

"Mrs. Endicott?" he asked, suddenly conscious that his chin would be rough with an eighteen-hour growth of beard.

"Yes, Officer, what can I do for you?"

Sam made a fast decision. "May I see Mr. Endicott, please?"

Grace Endicott stepped back and held the door open. "Come in," she invited. "I'll get him for you."

Sam walked in, conscious of being out of his element. He followed his hostess into a long, bright living room, the left wall of which was almost entirely glass. The opposite wall was covered with long shelves that reached from floor to ceiling and held the largest collection of books and record albums that Sam had ever seen.

"Sit down, won't you, please," Mrs. Endicott invited, and then walked quickly from the room. Sam looked about him at the big, comfortable-looking chairs and decided to remain on his feet. He told himself that it would be all over in ten minutes, maybe even less, and then he could get back into his car and drive down into town once more.

Sam turned as his host walked into the room. Endicott showed his age more than did his wife, but he carried his years with a calm dignity. He belonged in his house, and the house in turn specifically belonged to him. They fitted each other as certain captains fit the ships which they command. While Sam waited for the man to speak, he wished for a moment that his position was such that he could have these people for his friends. Then he remembered what he had to do.

"I believe you wished to see me." Endicott made it an invitation.

"Yes, sir. I believe you know a Mr. Mantoli?" Sam knew it wasn't good, but he had started now, and couldn't retreat.

"Yes, we know Maestro Mantoli very well. I hope he is not in any trouble?"

Sam reached up and removed his uniform cap, ashamed that he had forgotten to do so until now. "Yes and no, Mr. Endicott." Sam flushed. There was nothing for it now but to state the facts. "I'm very sorry to have to tell you...that he has been killed."

Endicott rested his hand for a moment on the back of a chair and then sank into it, his eyes focused far away. "Enrico dead. I can't believe it." Sam stood awkwardly still and waited for Endicott to recover himself.

"This is dreadful, Officer," Endicott said finally. "He was our close and dear friend; his daughter is a guest here now. I..." Sam cursed the day he had left his job at the garage to become a police officer. Then Endicott turned to him. "How did the accident happen?" he asked very quietly.

This time Sam found better words. "Unfortunately, sir, it was not an accident. Mr. Mantoli was attacked early this morning in the downtown area. We don't know yet by whom or how. I found his body around four this morning." Sam wanted to say something else. "I'm terribly sorry to have to bring you this news," he added, hoping that the words would somehow help to lessen the shock to the man who sat before him.

"You mean," Endicott said very carefully, "he was murdered."

Sam nodded, grateful that he didn't have to put it into words.

Endicott rose. "I had better tell my wife," he said. To Sam it seemed as if the man had suddenly grown tired, not the weariness of a single day, but the kind of fatigue that sinks into the bones and remains there like a disease.

"Sit down, please," Endicott asked, and walked slowly out of the beautifully appointed room. Sam could feel the emptiness in the air when he had gone.

Sam let himself down until he was perched on the front six inches of one of the deep, comfortable chairs. In that position he was half sitting, half squatting, but the posture suited his mood. He tried to put out of his mind the scene that would be taking place in another part of the house. He looked hard through the glass wall at the spectacular view, which had about it a suggestion of eternity.

Endicott came back into the room. "Is there something specific I can do to help?" he asked.

Sam pulled himself to his feet. "Yes, sir. I—that is, we understood that Mr. Mantoli's daughter was staying here. We thought she ought to be notified. Later, when she feels able to, we would like to have her come down and formally identify the body."

Endicott hesitated a moment. "Miss Mantoli is here; she is still resting. We were all up very late last night making final plans for the music festival." He passed his hand across his forehead. "When Miss Mantoli wakes up, my wife will break the news to her. Meanwhile, is there any reason why I can't make the identification? I would like to spare her that if I could."

"I'm sure you can do that," Sam answered. He tried to speak sympathetically, but he could not seem to shape the sounds as he wanted them to come out. "If you would like, you can come down with me now. An officer will bring you back."

"All right," Endicott said. "Let me tell my wife and I'll be right with you."

As he drove back down the winding road, with Endicott by his side, Sam kept his eyes on the road and measured every movement of the controls to keep the car in steady, even motion. He was still driving with extra care when he pulled up in front of the police entrance of the municipal building and discharged his passenger. Then he followed a step behind as the older man climbed the steps that led up to the lobby and the desk.

Sam had planned to bow out at that point and ask permission to go home. When Endicott turned to follow Arnold to the morgue, he changed his mind and walked beside the older man in the hope that by so doing he might lend him some moral strength. He hated the moment when the sheet was turned back and Endicott weakly nodded his head.

"That is the body of Maestro Enrico Mantoli," he said, and then, his duty done, he turned quickly to go. Back in the lobby, he made a request. "May I see your police chief?" he asked.

Fred, at the desk, spoke into an intercom. A moment later he nodded, and Sam, sensing his role, led the way. "Mr. Endicott, this is Chief Gillespie," he said after they reached the office.

Endicott held out his hand. "We have met," he said simply. "I am a member of the city council."

Gillespie got to his feet and came out quickly from behind his desk. "Of course, Mr. Endicott. Thank you very much for coming down." He started back to his chair and then turned around. "Please sit down," he invited.

George Endicott seated himself carefully in the hard oak chair. "Chief Gillespie," he began, "I know that you and your department will do everything possible to find and punish the person who did this. Whatever I can do to help, I want you to call on me. Maestro Mantoli was our very good friend; we brought him here. To that extent we brought him to his death. I think you understand how I feel."

Gillespie reached for a pad of paper and plucked a

41

pen out of his desk set. "Perhaps you can give me a few facts now," he suggested. "How old was the deceased, do you know?"

"Enrico was forty-seven."

"Married?"

"Widowed."

"Next of kin?"

"His daughter, Duena, his only child. She is our house guest now."

"Nationality?"

"He was an American citizen."

Gillespie frowned very slightly, then cleared his features consciously. "Where was he born?" he asked.

Endicott hesitated. "Somewhere in Italy. I can't remember exactly."

"Genoa, I believe," Virgil Tibbs supplied quietly.

Both men turned to look at him; Endicott spoke first. "You were a friend of Maestro Mantoli's?" he asked.

"No, I never had the honor of meeting him. But at Chief Gillespie's invitation, I examined his body this morning."

Endicott looked puzzled. "You are a...mortician?" he suggested.

Tibbs shook his head. Before he could speak, Gillespie intervened. "Virgil here is a police investigator out in Beverly Hills, California."

"Pasadena," Tibbs corrected.

"All right then, Pasadena. What difference does it make?" Gillespie let his temper edge his voice.

George Endicott got to his feet. "I haven't heard your name," he said, and held out his hand.

The young Negro rose and took it. "My name is Tibbs."

"I'm happy to know you, Mr. Tibbs," Endicott acknowledged. "What type of investigation do you do?"

"Quite a variety, sir, I've done some narcotics work

42

for the vice division, traffic work, and burglary, but I specialize in crimes against persons—homicide, rape, and similar major offenses."

Endicott turned toward Gillespie. "How does it happen that Mr. Tibbs is here?" he asked.

When Sam Wood saw the look that was forming on Gillespie's face, he realized it was up to him. "I'm responsible," he admitted. "I found Virgil waiting for a train and brought him in as a possible suspect. Then we found out who he was."

"Officer Wood acted very promptly," Tibbs added. "He didn't take any chances of letting a possible murderer get away."

At that moment, for the first time in his life, Sam Wood found himself liking a Negro.

Endicott spoke again to the Pasadena detective. "How long are you going to be in Wells?" he asked.

"Until the next train," Tibbs answered.

"And when is that?"

"If I remember, three-forty this afternoon."

Endicott nodded that he was satisfied. Gillespie shifted uncomfortably in his chair. It occurred to Sam Wood that this was the time to leave. Gradually it was dawning on him that his chief was on a spot and that he had put him there. He cleared his throat to give notice that he intended to speak. "Sir," he said to Gillespie, "if I can be spared now, I'd like to clean up and get some rest."

Gillespie glanced up. "Go on home," he said.

As Sam Wood settled himself behind the wheel of his four-year-old Plymouth, he began to think about the obvious tension between Bill Gillespie and the Negro detective. There was no question in his mind who would win out, but he was disturbed by the growing feeling that if things broke the wrong way, he could be caught in the middle.

Still churning over this sobering thought, he parked the car in front of his small house, let himself in, lost no time in taking off his clothes, and showered. For a moment he contemplated getting something to eat. Then he decided he wasn't hungry and climbed into bed. He pulled a single sheet over his body in lieu of pajamas and, despite the broiling heat and his disturbed state of mind, went immediately to sleep.

— 5 —

As soon as Endicott had left his office and was safely out of the corridor, Bill Gillespie turned toward Virgil Tibbs.

"Who in hell asked you to open your big black mouth," he demanded. "If I want you to tell me anything, I'll ask you. I was questioning Endicott exactly the way I wanted to until you butted in." He clenched his massive right hand into a fist and rubbed it in the palm of his left. "Now get this—I want you out of here right now. I don't know when the next train is and I don't care; go down to the station and wait for it. When it comes in, never mind which way it's going, just get on. Beat it!"

Virgil Tibbs rose quietly to his feet. He walked to the door of the office, turned, and looked directly into the face of the big man who dominated the small room. "Good morning, Chief Gillespie," he said. As he walked through the outer lobby, the desk man stopped him.

"Virgil, did you leave a brown fiber-glass suitcase in the station this morning? Initials V.R.T. on it?"

Tibbs nodded. "Yes, that's mine. Where is it?"

"We've got it. Wait five minutes till I finish this and I'll get it for you."

Tibbs waited uncomfortably; he did not want Gillespie to come out of his office and find him still there. He was not afraid of the big man, but he saw no possible advantage in another scene. He stayed on his feet to suggest politely that he was expecting the wait to be a short one.

After a long five minutes, the desk man returned with his bag. "Can I get a ride to the station?" Tibbs asked.

"Go ask the chief. If he OK's it, it's fine with me."

"Never mind," Tibbs answered shortly. He picked up his bag and began to walk down the long flight of steps that led to the street.

Nine minutes later, the phone rang in Gillespie's office. It was his private line, the number of which was known to only a few people. He picked up the instrument. "Gillespie," he acknowledged tersely.

"This is Frank Schubert, Bill."

"Yes, Frank." The chief made an effort to sound confident and cordial. Frank Schubert ran a hardware store and owned two gas stations. He was also the mayor of Wells and the chairman of the small committee which ran the city's affairs.

"Bill, George Endicott just left my office."

"Yes," Gillespie almost shouted, and resolved to keep his voice under better control.

"It was about this colored detective that one of your boys spaded up. He wanted me to call Pasadena and ask if we could borrow him for a few days. George is terribly upset about Mantoli's death, you know."

"I know that, too," Gillespie cut in. He felt he was being treated like a child.

"We got through immediately to Chief Morris in Pasadena," Schubert went on. "He gave us his OK."

Gillespie gulped a deep breath. "Frank, I appreciate your effort very much, but I just got rid of that guy and frankly, I don't want him back. I have good people here and I'm not inexperienced myself. Excuse my saying this to you, but Endicott is a meddler."

"I know he is," Schubert agreed, "and he comes from up North, where they think differently than we do. But I think you're overlooking something."

"What's that?" Gillespie asked.

"The fact that this gives you a perfect out. Endicott wants us to use his black friend. OK, go ahead and do it. Suppose he finds the man you want? He has no police power here, so he will have to hand the whole thing over to you. But if he fails, that lets you completely off the hook. And everybody in town will be with you; the whole blame goes to him. Either way you win. If you don't use him and for any reason fail to nail your murderer in fairly short order, Endicott will be out for your scalp, and he's got more dough than anybody else in this town."

Gillespie chewed on his lower lip for a moment. "I just kicked him out of here," he said.

"You better get him back," Schubert warned. "He's your alibi. Be nice to him and let him hang himself. If anybody blames you, say that you did it on my orders."

Gillespie knew then that he was hooked. "All right," he said in an unwilling voice, and hung up. He got up quickly, reminding himself that he didn't know the first thing about the procedure in catching a murderer and that Virgil Tibbs was the unwitting alibi that would lift the whole responsibility from his shoulders. By the time he jackknifed himself into his car, he had decided that it would be good to give Tibbs the rope with which to hang himself.

Two blocks from the station he found his man. Tibbs had paused for a moment to switch his suitcase from one hand to the other as Gillespie slid his car up to the curb. "Virgil, get in, I want to talk to you," he said.

As the young Negro moved to obey, Gillespie had a sudden revolting thought. Tibbs had been walking and carrying a heavy bag for some blocks in the hot sun. That meant he would be sweating and Gillespie hated the odor he associated with black men. He reached around and quickly rolled down the rear window behind him. As soon as that was done, he motioned Tibbs to come in the front seat. "Put your bag in back," he instructed. Tibbs did as directed, climbed into the car, and sat down. To Gillespie's intense relief, he didn't smell.

Gillespie started the car and moved out into traffic. "Virgil," he began, "I was a little rough on you this morning." It occurred to him to stop right there and he did.

Tibbs said nothing.

"Your friend Endicott," Gillespie went on, "spoke to our mayor about you. Mayor Schubert phoned Pasadena. After consulting with me, we reached a decision to have you investigate Mantoli's murder under my direction."

There was silence in the car for the next three blocks. Then Tibbs broke it carefully. "I think, Chief Gillespie, that it might be better if I left town as you suggested. It might make things easier for you."

Gillespie swung the car around a corner. "What would you do if your boss asked you to stay here?" he inquired.

"If Chief Morris asked me to," Tibbs replied promptly, "I'd go to England and look for Jack the Ripper."

"Chief Morris sent word to you to spend a week here with us. You won't be a member of our department, of course, so you won't be able to wear a uniform."

"I haven't for some time," Tibbs said.

"OK. What do you think you will need?"

"I have been up all night and haven't had a chance

to clean up," Tibbs answered. "If there is a hotel here that will take me, I'd like to shave, shower, and put on some clean clothes. Then if you can fix me up with some sort of transportation, that will be about all I'll need. At least for a while."

Gillespie thought for a moment. "The hotels here won't take you, Virgil, but there is a motel for colored about five miles up the road. You can stay there. We've got an old police car in reserve I could let you have."

"Please," Tibbs requested, "not a police car. If you know a used-car dealer who will lend me something that runs, that would be a lot better. I don't want to be conspicuous."

Gillespie realized that it was going to be harder to make Tibbs undo himself than he thought. "I think I know a place," he said, and U-turned in the middle of the block. He drove to a garage on the other side of the railroad tracks. A huge Negro mechanic came out to meet him.

"Jess," Gillespie instructed, "this is Virgil, who is working for me. I want you to lend him a car or get him one he can use. For a week or so. Something that runs all right, something maybe you've fixed up."

"Anything I fix up," Jess replied, "runs right. Who'll be responsible?"

"I will," Tibbs said.

"Come on, then," Jess retorted, and walked back into his shop. Virgil Tibbs got out of Gillespie's car, pulled his bag from the rear seat, and spoke to his new superior. "I'll report in as soon as I can clean up," he said.

"Take your time," Gillespie answered. "Tomorrow will be all right." He pushed hard on the gas pedal and the car jumped away, throwing up a cloud of dust. Virgil Tibbs picked up his suitcase and walked into the garage.

"Who are you?" Jess asked.

"My name is Tibbs. I'm a policeman from California."

Jess wiped his hands on a garage rag. "I'm saving up to move west myself. I want to get out of here," he confided, "but don't tell nobody. You can take my car. I got another one to drive if I need it. What are you supposed to be doing?"

"They had a murder here this morning. They don't know what to do about it, so they're using me for a fall guy."

A look of heavy suspicion crossed Jess's round black face. "How you gonna protect yourself?" he asked.

"By catching the murderer," Tibbs answered.

Because of the heat, and the upsetting of his routine, Sam Wood had a short and fitful sleep. By two in the afternoon he was up and dressed. He made himself a sandwich from the simple provisions he kept on hand and then read his mail. The last of the three letters in the small pile he opened with shaking fingers. There was a note on a legal letterhead and a check. When he looked at the check, Sam stopped worrying about the murder. He shoved the letter and check into his breast pocket, looked at his watch, and hurried out of his house. Suddenly it was important to him to reach the bank before three.

An hour later, Sam drove to the police station to pick up the news. It was also payday. To his amazement he found Bill Gillespie in the lobby talking to Virgil Tibbs.

Sam picked up his pay check at the desk, signed for it, and then turned to find Bill Gillespie waiting for him. "Wood, I know you're off duty, but we need some help around here. Can you drive Virgil up to the Endicotts'; he wants to interview Mantoli's daughter." It was not a question, but a moderately put order. Sam did not understand the sudden toleration of the California detective, but discretion told him not to pick that time and place to ask. He was glad to go; he didn't want to miss anything.

"Certainly, Chief, if you want me to."

Gillespie drew an exasperated breath. "If I didn't want you to, Wood, I wouldn't have asked you. Virgil has a car, but you know the way."

Why was it, Sam asked himself, that every time he tried to be courteous to Gillespie, his new chief took it the wrong way. He nodded to Tibbs and wondered for an instant if he should drive his personal car up the mountain or use his regular patrol car, which was parked in the yard. He was not in uniform. The solution leaped into his mind: he was for a moment a plainclothesman; as such he would drive the official car. He led the way, Tibbs followed. When Sam climbed into the driver's seat, Tibbs opened the opposite door and sat beside him. After a moment's hesitation, Sam accepted the arrangement and pressed the starter.

When they were out of traffic and moving through the outskirts toward the road that led up to the Endicott aerie, Sam yielded to his curiosity. "You seem to have gotten on the good side of the chief," he remarked, then wondered immediately if he had been too friendly, too overt, or both.

"I know you must have been wondering," Tibbs responded. "My presence here embarrassed Chief Gillespie and I had the bad judgment to intrude myself into an interview he was conducting."

"I know," Sam said.

Tibbs took no offense. "Without going into details, Chief Gillespie has assigned me to help on the Mantoli case for a few days. This is with the approval and permission of my superiors at home."

"What's your status, then?" Sam asked curiously.

"None, except that I'm going to be allowed to try my hand. I may hang myself in the process."

The car reached the end of the pavement and hit the gravel.

"Think you can do any good?" Sam asked.

"I can give you some references," Tibb answered.

"They can't do you much good here if they're in California," Sam pointed out.

"They're in California," Tibbs acknowledged. "San Quentin."

Sam decided to shut up and drive.

When the door of the Endicott house swung open to him for the second time that day, Mrs. Endicott was there as before. She had changed into a simple black dress. Although she did not smile, she made him feel welcome. "I'm glad to see you, Officer," she said. "I'm sorry I don't know your name."

"It's Sam Wood, ma'am."

She offered him her hand briefly. "And this gentleman I'm sure is Mr. Tibbs." She gave the Negro her hand for a moment. "Please come in, gentlemen," she invited.

Sam followed his hostess into the big, spectacular living room; as he entered he saw not only Endicott, but also a younger man and a girl. They were holding hands and Sam sensed at once that it was his idea, not hers. The men stood up for introductions.

"Duena, may I present Mr. Tibbs and Mr. Wood; Miss Mantoli. And Mr. Eric Kaufmann, Maestro Mantoli's associate and manager."

The men shook hands. Sam immediately did not care much for Kaufmann. He was a youngish man who looked as if he was trying to be older, taller, and more important than he was.

The girl was different. As she sat, quietly composed, Sam took a quick, careful look and revised drastically his estimate of Italian women. This one was not fat and did not look as though she ever would be. She was dark, he noted, with the type of short-cropped hair which had always appealed to him. He reminded himself that this girl had learned only that morning that her father had been brutally murdered. He felt an impulse to sit beside her, to put his arm gently across her shoulders and tell her that somehow everything was going to be all right.

But it couldn't possibly be all right for her—not for a long time to come. He was still thinking about her when Virgil Tibbs calmly took command.

"Miss Mantoli," Tibbs said, "we have only one excuse for disturbing you at a time like this: we need your help to find and punish the person responsible. Do you feel able to answer some questions?"

The girl looked at him for a moment with eyes that were red-rimmed and liquid, then she shut them and nodded silently toward chairs. Sam sat down with a strong sense of relief; he wanted very much to fade into the background and let Tibbs handle things.

"Perhaps it would be easiest if I began with you," Tibbs said as he turned toward Eric Kaufmann. "Were you here last night?"

"Yes, I was, for the first part of the evening, that is. I had to leave at ten in order to drive to Atlanta. It's a long way from here and I had to be there early in the morning."

"Did you drive all night?" Tibbs asked.

"Oh, no; I got in about two-thirty in the morning. I checked into my hotel there to get some sleep, at least. I was up and shaving when...when the call came through," he finished.

Tibbs turned to the girl, who sat with her head down, her hands held tightly together in front of her knees. When he spoke, his voice changed a little in timbre.

It was quiet and matter-of-fact, but it showed an undercurrent of sympathy for the unhappy girl who sat before him.

"Were there any unsuccessful candidates for the position your father held who might have been . . . greatly upset by his success?" he asked.

The girl looked up. "None at all," she answered. She spoke softly, but her words were clear, distinct, and unafraid. She had no accent whatever. "I mean really none at all. The festival here was his idea and there was never anyone else . . ." She let her voice trail off and did not attempt to finish the sentence.

"Did your father normally carry considerable sums of money with him—say, over two hundred dollars?"

"Sometimes, for traveling expenses. I tried to get him to use traveler's checks, but he found them too much bother." She looked up and asked a question of her own. "Was that what he was killed for—a few dollars?" she asked. There was bitterness in her voice and her lips seemed to quiver as she spoke. Her eyes grew wet again.

"I very much doubt it, Miss Mantoli," Tibbs answered her. "There are three other strong possibilities, at least, that will have to be investigated. But I don't think it was that."

Grace Endicott interrupted. "Mr. Tibbs, I appreciate what you are doing for us, but may I make a suggestion: perhaps we can answer most of your questions between us and spare Duena. The shock has been a terrible thing for her; I know you understand that."

"Of course I do," Tibbs acknowledged. "After Miss Mantoli has had a chance to recover somewhat, I can talk to her—if I need to."

Grace Endicott held out her hand to the girl. "Come on in and lie down," she invited.

The girl stood up, but shook her head. "I'd rather

go outside for a little while," she said. "I know it's hot, but I want to go outside. Please."

The older woman understood. "I'll get you a hat," she suggested, "something to protect your head from the sun. You'll need that." As the two women left the room, George Endicott said, "I don't like her out there alone. We're well isolated up here, but until this thing is cleared up, I don't want to take any chances—none whatsoever. Eric, would you please..." Then he stopped.

Sam Wood felt something pulse through him that he had never experienced before. Quietly he got to his feet. "Let me go with her," he volunteered. He was almost twice Kaufmann's size and he was an officer of the law, in uniform or not. The responsibility was his.

"I'm perfectly capable—" Kaufmann began.

"You will probably be needed here," George Endicott reminded him. Sam took this to mean his offer had been accepted. He nodded to Endicott and walked toward the front door. He knew there would be no danger outside in the bright light of day, and he almost regretted it. He would have preferred to have been in uniform so that his weapon would be conspicuously in sight to give the girl confidence. As it was, he was simply a good-size man in a business suit. Grace Endicott reappeared with Duena Mantoli. The girl had on a large-brimmed summer hat in which, despite her evident grief, she looked almost improperly attractive. Sam drew in his breath.

"I'll escort Miss Mantoli," he announced firmly.

"Thank you," Grace Endicott replied. Sam held the door open so that the girl could walk outside.

Without speaking, Duena Mantoli led the way around the house and to the beginning of a little footpath on the opposite side from the entrance drive. It led down the hillside at a gentle angle for two or three hundred feet and ended at a little roofed lookout platform which Sam had not known was there. It was set in an indentation in the hillside so that it was screened from above and both sides, with a bench seat built at its rear so that anyone who wished to could sit there unobserved and look out over the Great Smokies.

Duena seated herself quietly and pulled her skirt over to indicate that Sam was permitted to sit beside her. Sam sat down, folded his hands, and looked out at the miles of country before him. He knew why the girl had come here: because this place seemed to be perched on the edge of the infinite; it was impossible to look out over the marching mountains and not feel that beyond the horizon they went on forever.

They sat quietly together for some moments; then, without preamble, the girl asked a question. "You found my father's body, didn't you?"

"Are you sure you want to talk about it?" Sam asked.

"I want to know," the girl answered him. "Did you find his body?"

"Yes, I did."

"Where was it?"

Sam hesitated before he answered. "In the middle of the highway."

"Could he have been struck by a car?"

"No." Sam paused, wondering how much more he should add. "He had been struck from behind with a blunt instrument. His stick was beside him—his cane, I mean. That might have been it."

"Was it"—the girl hesitated and chose her words carefully—"instantaneous?" For the first time she turned her head and looked at him.

Sam nodded. "Not only that, but he had no knowledge, I'm sure, no pain."

The girl gripped the edge of the bench with long, slender fingers and looked out once more at the mountain panorama before her. "He wasn't a big man, or important," she said half to the silent hills. "All his life he hoped and worked for the big break. This would have been it, his chance to be somebody in music. It's a hard world and it's almost impossible to get anywhere unless you somehow manage to belong to just the right group. Whoever killed my father killed all of his hopes and dreams—just before they were all to have come true." She stopped speaking, but she continued to stare straight ahead. Sam looked at her carefully and was angry with himself for, at a time like this, deciding she was beautiful. He wanted desperately to offer her his protection, to let her cry on his ample shoulder if she wanted to, to hold her hand in a reassuring grip.

What he could not do physically, he tried to do with words. "Miss Mantoli, I want to tell you something that may help, just a little. All of us in the police department are going to do our best, no matter how hard we have to work, to find and punish the person responsible. That isn't much comfort for you, but it might help a little."

"You're very kind, Mr. Wood," she said, as though she was really thinking of something else. "Is Mr. Tibbs's being here going to cause you any trouble?" she asked abruptly.

Sam wrinkled his brow for a moment. "Truthfully, that's hard to answer. I honestly don't know."

"Because he's a Negro."

"Yes, because he's black. You know how we feel about things like that down here."

When the girl looked at him steadily and evenly, Sam felt a sudden emotion he could not analyze. "I know," she said. "Some people don't like Italians; they think we're different, you know. Oh, they'll make an exception for a Toscanini or a Sophia Loren, but the rest of us are supposed to be vegetable peddlers or else

57

gangsters." She pushed back her hair carelessly with one hand, looked away from him out over the mountains.

"Perhaps we ought to go back," Sam suggested, acutely uncomfortable.

The girl rose to her feet. "I suppose so. Thank you for coming with me," she said. "It helped."

As they reached the door of the house, it opened and Eric Kaufmann appeared. He held it open for Virgil Tibbs, who followed him, and then made a particular point of carefully shaking hands. Even Sam realized it was formal patronizing. "Mr. Tibbs," Kaufmann said in a voice loud enough for Sam and the girl to hear, "I don't care what it costs or what you have to do. I'm not a rich man, but I'll stop at nothing to see that the murder—that the person who did what he did to the maestro is captured and made to pay." His voice broke. "To strike him down like that, a man like him! Not even to give him a chance. Please, do your very best!"

Sam wondered how much of the speech was sincere and how much was calculated to impress the girl. He must know her well, Sam thought, and perhaps...He did not let himself finish the thought. Unreasonably he wished that the girl had somehow risen out of the ground that day so that he might be the first to know her and to take care of her.

He decided he was losing his grip and it was time to toughen up.

Virgil Tibbs excused himself and they climbed into the car. Sam started the engine and turned down the road that led back to the city. When they were safely out of range of the house, he spoke. "Did you make any progress?"

"Yes, I did," Tibbs answered him.

Sam waited for a fuller explanation, then found he had to ask for one. "Such as what, Virgil?"

"Mostly background on Mantoli and the music festival. The Endicotts are strong local sponsors. What they had set up here was what they hoped would develop into another Tanglewood or the Bethlehem Bach Festival. Some projects of that kind have been highly successful."

"Most of us around here regarded the whole thing as being nuts," Sam said.

"The response from the advance announcements was surprisingly good," Tibbs added. "I don't know too much about music, but apparently Mantoli had arranged some special programs that had a lot of appeal to the kind of people who come to things like this. At least they were willing to pay good money to sit on logs or camp chairs for a whole evening until the thing was proved a success and something better put in."

"How about something that will help us with the problem we've got right now? Anything that might point to who did it?"

"Possibly," Tibbs answered vaguely. He added, "Mr. Endicott has asked to have Mantoli's body moved to the undertaker's as soon as possible."

Sam waited a moment and then gave up. "What next?" he asked.

"Let's go back to the station. I want to see that fellow Oberst they're holding there."

"I forgot about him," Sam confessed. "What are you going to do to him?"

"I want to talk to him," Tibbs answered. "After that a lot depends on how much leeway Gillespie is going to give me."

They drove the rest of the way in silence. As he guided the car down the turns of the winding road, Sam tried to decide whether or not he wanted the man sitting beside him to succeed in what he had undertaken. In his mind he saw a clear picture of Duena

59

Mantoli; then, as a projector shifts slides, he saw Gillespie and, without looking at him, the Negro by his side. That was what hurt. An outsider might be all right if he were a good fellow and all that, but the idea of a black man stuck up like a jagged rock in the middle of a channel. By the time they had reached the police station, Sam had still not made up his mind. He wanted the crime solved, but he wanted it solved by someone whom he could look up to and respect. The only trouble was he couldn't think who it might be.

— 6 —

Virgil Tibbs stopped at the desk and made a request. Then he disappeared in the direction of the colored washroom to allow time for it to be considered and for Gillespie to be consulted. The chief was out of the building so the desk man had to make his own decision. After recalling his instructions carefully, he made up his mind, called Arnold, and asked him to admit Tibbs to Harvey Oberst's cell.

When the steel door swung partly open, Oberst half rose to his feet. "You don't have to put him in here," he protested. "Put him someplace else. I don't want no nig—"

The steel door clanked shut. "He wants to talk to you," Arnold said acidly, and left. Oberst sank down on one extreme end of the hard board bunk, Tibbs seated himself calmly on the other. He had taken off his coat and tie and had rolled up his sleeves. He folded his lean, dark fingers in his lap and sat silently, paying no attention to Oberst. The minutes passed unnoticed as neither man made any attempt to do anything. Then Oberst began to fidget. First he moved his hands, then he began to shuffle his feet. After a period of increasing nervousness he found his voice and spoke. "What you doing with white man's clothes on?" he asked.

For the first time Tibbs appeared to notice that Oberst was present. "I bought them from a white man," he answered.

Harvey Oberst turned his attention now to his cellmate and looked him up and down with unconcealed appraisal. "You been to school?" he asked.

Tibbs nodded slowly. "College."

Oberst bristled. "You think you're smart or something?"

Virgil Tibbs continued to look at his locked fingers. "I graduated."

The silence returned for a moment.

"Where'd they let you go to college?"

"In California."

Oberst shifted his position and lifted his feet up onto the hard surface of the bunk. "Out there they don't care what they do."

Tibbs ignored the comment. "Who's Delores Purdy?" he asked.

Oberst leaned forward. "None of your business," he snapped. "She's a white girl."

Tibbs unfolded his hands, swung around, and put his own feet on the bunk exactly as Oberst had done. "Either you answer my question," he said, "or take your chances on being hanged for murder."

"Don't you give me any of your lip, black boy," Harvey snarled. "You ain't nobody and you ain't never going to be nobody. High school or college don't make you white and you know it."

"I don't especially want to be white," Tibbs said, "but white or black, it doesn't make much difference when you're at the end of a rope. And after you've rotted for a few months in the ground—say, a little more than a year from now—no one will know or care what color your skin was. You won't have a skin anymore. Is that the way you want it?"

Oberst pulled his knees up close to his chest and

clasped his arms around them as though to protect himself. "Who the hell do you think you are?" he demanded. But there was fear in his voice and the arrogance with which he tried to replace it didn't come off.

"I'm a cop. I'm after the man who killed the one you robbed. Whether you believe it or not, that's so. I also happen to be the only one around here who thinks you might not be guilty of murder. So you'd better back me up because I'm the best chance you've got."

"You ain't no cop," Oberst said after a pause.

Tibbs reached in his shirt pocket and pulled out a small white card sealed in plastic. "I work in Pasadena; I'm an investigator. Call it detective if you like. I've been loaned to the police department to find out who killed Mantoli—that's the dead man you found. Never mind how or why. Either you gamble on me or stand trial for murder."

Oberst remained silent.

Tibbs waited a long minute. "Who is Delores Purdy?" he asked again.

Oberst made his decision. "She's a girl who lives near where I do. One of a whole flock of kids."

"How old is she?"

"Sixteen, almost seventeen."

"You know what we call that kind in California? San Quentin quail," Tibbs said.

Oberst reacted quickly. "I got in trouble with her, but not that way."

"What happened?"

Oberst didn't answer.

"I can go out and look up the record," Tibbs reminded him. "I'd rather get it from you."

Oberst accepted defeat. "This Delores, she's young but real stacked, if you know what I mean. A real hot sweater-girl type."

"There're lots of those," Tibbs commented.

"Yeah, but this Delores is real proud of what nature done for her. She likes to show off. I took her on a date to Clarke's Pond. We weren't plannin' nothing wrong; I don't want to join no chain gang."

Tibbs nodded.

"Anyhow, she asks me if I don't think she's got a nice figure, and when I say yes, she decides to show me."

"It was her idea?" Tibbs asked.

"Like you said, her idea. I didn't mess her up or anything like that; I just didn't try to stop her."

"Not too many people would blame you for that, but it was pretty dangerous."

"Maybe so. Anyhow, she gets half undressed and right then a cop comes out of the bushes. I get hauled in."

"How about the girl?"

"She got sent home."

"What happened after that?"

"After a while they let me go, told me never to mess around with that girl anymore."

"Have you seen her since?"

"Sure, she lives on Third Street at the corner of Polk. I live half a block from there. I see her all the time. She wants another date."

"That's all that happened?"

"Nothin' else, so help me."

Tibbs got to his feet, took hold of the bars of the cell and swung his weight backward so as to pull at the cramped muscles of his arms. Then he walked back and sat down again.

"Do you shave every day?" he asked.

Surprised, Oberst felt his chin. "Usually I do. I didn't this morning; I been up all night."

"How come?"

64

"I went to Canville to see a guy I know there. We...had a couple of dates."

"Then you got back here pretty late?"

"Sometime around two, maybe later. That's when I found the guy in the road."

"Exactly what did you do? Don't tell me what you think I want to hear; just tell me what really happened."

"Well, this here guy was lying on his face on the road. I stopped to see if I could help him. But he was dead."

"How did you know?"

"Well, I just knew, that's all."

"Go on."

"Well, I seen his wallet lying on the road, maybe four or five feet from him."

Virgil Tibbs leaned forward. "That's very important," he emphasized. "I don't care whether you found the wallet or whether you took it out of his pocket, it makes no difference. But are you absolutely sure you found it on the road beside him?"

"I swear I did," Oberst answered.

"Then you did," Tibbs conceded. "What happened after that?"

"I picked it up and looked quick inside. I seen a lot of money. I figured he couldn't use it anymore, and if I left it there, whoever came along next would grab it."

"That's probably right," Tibbs agreed. "Now how did you get caught with it on you?"

"Well, I got worried about it on account of the guy had been killed. If anybody found me with the wallet, I could be in awful bad trouble. So I went to see Mr. Jennings. He's head man at the bank and I know him because I work for him weekends. I told him about it. He said it would have to be reported and he called the cops. So I got stuck in here anyway. Now I don't know what I'll get."

Tibbs got to his feet. "Leave it to me," he advised. "If your story holds up, you're all right." He called loudly enough to be heard and waited for Arnold to come and let him out.

Shortly thereafter Tibbs went to the weather bureau and checked the rainfall records for the last month.

Bill Gillespie looked up from his desk to see his new assistant from Pasadena standing in the doorway. He did not want to see Virgil Tibbs; he did not want to see anybody. He wanted to go home, wash up, get something to eat, and go to bed. It was late in the working day and he had been on duty since the very early hours of the morning.

"Well, what is it?" he demanded.

Tibbs walked in a short way, but did not sit down. "Since you put me in charge of the investigation of Mantoli's death, Chief Gillespie, I'd like to ask you to release Harvey Oberst."

"Why?" Gillespie made the question a challenge.

"He's not guilty of the murder, I'm sure of that, and for more reasons than I gave you this morning. Technically you could hold him for grand theft for taking the wallet, but I checked with Mr. Jennings at the bank and he confirmed Oberst's story that he turned the wallet in to him—at least he asked Jennings' advice about it. With a responsible citizen to testify, you'd never get a conviction against Oberst."

Gillespie waved one hand to show that he assumed no responsibility. "All right, let him go. It's your responsibility. He looked like a good suspect to me."

"I don't want a suspect," Tibbs replied. "I want a murderer. Oberst, I'm sure, isn't our man. Thank you, sir."

66

As Tibbs left the room, Gillespie noted with some satisfaction that at least he had known enough to say "sir." He got up and scowled at the papers on his desk. Then he shrugged his shoulders and walked out through the lobby. It was Virgil's responsibility and whatever else happened, he, Gillespie, was in the clear.

At a few minutes past midnight, Sam Wood climbed into his patrol car, checked the gas gauge to be sure the tank had been filled, and drove out of the police parking lot. He had ahead of him eight hours alone with the city, which would soon be asleep. But things were different tonight. Somewhere, probably still within the city, there was a killer. A killer to whom human life was not as important as something he wanted.

Tonight, Sam resolved, as he swung west on his accustomed route, he would keep his eyes and ears open as he had never done before. He let his imagination take hold briefly while he visualized trapping and catching a murderer so clearly guilty of his crime that it would show the moment he marched him into the police station.

But it didn't work that way, Sam told himself. Everything was on the killer's side. He could hide where he chose, unknown and unseen, strike at a time and place of his own choosing. Perhaps, Sam thought, the unknown killer might seize on the idea that somehow he, Sam, had seen too much. In that case the killer would be out for him—tonight. Sam reached down carefully and for the first time since he had put on a police uniform, loosened his sidearm in its holster. It would be a long eight hours.

As the car wove westward through the already silent and deserted streets, Sam had a sudden idea. To put it into effect might be dangerous and it would be definitely exceeding his authority. It might even be called a neglect of duty. Despite all of these objections, he knew almost at once he was going to do it anyway. He swung the car around a corner and headed for the dirt road that led up to the Endicott place.

When the wheels of the car bit into the gravel, Sam was as calmly determined as he had ever been in his life. Mantoli was dead; no one knew why. Whatever the reason, it might apply also to his daughter. Sam thought of the girl who had sat beside him looking out over the mountains, and almost wished that the killer would prowl again tonight, but not until he, Sam, got there first.

As the road climbed upward, the air seemed to grow cooler and cleaner. Sam switched on the bright lights and swung the car expertly around the curves of the semiprivate road.

It was a flicker of light against a white guard rail that first told him that another car was coming in the opposite direction.

At a point where the road widened slightly, Sam pulled over, switched his headlights to parking position, and waited. He reached for the flashlight that was clipped to the steering column and held it ready in his left hand. The headlights of the approaching car threw a brighter loom into the sky; as they came into view, Sam, on impulse, switched on his red spotlight. The driver of the other car hit his brakes and pulled up opposite. Sam stabbed him with the beam of the flashlight, and as the driver threw up his arm to shield his eyes, Sam recognized Eric Kaufmann.

"What are you doing on this road at this hour?" Sam demanded.

"I'm on my way to Atlanta. Why?" Sam sensed antagonism in the voice and he didn't like it.

"Is this the hour you usually start trips to Atlanta?"

Kaufmann leaned partway out of the car window. "Is that any business of yours?" he asked.

Sam stepped quickly from his car and stood beside Kaufmann, his right hand resting on the butt of his sidearm. "In case you have forgotten," he said, biting each word off separately, "less than twenty-four hours ago someone committed a murder in this town. Until we catch him, everyone's business is our concern, especially when they start out on long drives past midnight. Now explain yourself."

Kaufmann rubbed his fingers across his face for a moment. "I'm sorry, Officer," he apologized. "I'm not myself and you know why. I was up at the Endicotts' discussing the festival until a few minutes ago. Because a good deal of local money has been advanced for this project, we decided that we have to go ahead despite the fact that Enrico is dead. If we let it ride for a year, we'll all be dead. I'm sorry—that's a bad choice of words." Kaufmann stopped and made an effort to collect himself. "Anyhow, I've got to go to Atlanta and see what can be done to locate a name conductor to take over. And I've got to arrange for the orchestra; it was all lined up but the news may have thrown everything off again."

Sam relaxed a little. "That's fine, but why leave at this hour? According to the story you told me and Virgil, you got very little sleep last night. You can't be in very good condition to drive."

"You're right about that," Kaufmann agreed. "I'm leaving, frankly, because I don't want to be in the way up there. Duena is sleeping in the only guest room and right now she needs all the rest and quiet she can get. The only sensible thing was for me to leave, drive out of town a little ways, and go to a motel. Then I can get an early start and be in the city by noon. Any objections?"

Sam knew that the story made sense and he didn't want to let his dislike of the man color his judgment. And he remembered that this lonely mountain road was not in his patrol area. In fact, he was neglecting that area right now. And if the killer should be prowling somewhere down there...

"How is everything on top of the hill?" he asked.

"All right. Strained, of course, but there's nothing wrong. Are you going up there? If you went up there now you'd disturb them and possibly give them a scare. I'd rather you didn't, if you don't mind."

Sam motioned Kaufmann to go on. "Be careful," he warned. "Get off the road as soon as you can and get some sleep. Otherwise you may end up in the morgue alongside your boss."

Kaufmann winced but didn't comment. "All right, I will. Follow me down if you like. But leave them alone up there; they've had all they can take for one day." He pushed the drive button on his station wagon and eased it back into the center of the downgrade. Sam stood silently until Kaufmann had gone well on ahead, then he turned his car cautiously on the narrow road and followed.

As he kept the car under control with second gear and brake, Sam reflected that Kaufmann and Duena were probably good friends. At least Kaufmann was in a position to see a lot of the girl, and the way those people traveled around, he probably had a monopoly. The thought made Sam mad. He had met the girl only once, on the day when her father had been murdered, and yet he felt he was entitled to an interest and to worry about her protection.

The wheels of the car hit the city pavement and the ride smoothed out. As it did, Sam brought his mind back to the murderer loose in the city. At least there was a good chance he was still in the city. The streets were silent and dark now except for the lonesome dots of light under the widely scattered street lamps. Once more Sam reminded himself that he was a prime target; the baking heat of the night began to be streaked with a kind of chill that hung in the blackness, waiting.

A while back, Sam had read a book about a situation something like this. The author had used a word to describe it, an odd and unusual word which Sam had dutifully looked up in the dictionary. He could not remember the word now, but it began with *m*, he was pretty sure of that. Whatever it was, what the word meant hung in the air now.

Sam was not a coward. Determined to do his duty, he made his complete patrol of the city. When he had finished, he took the precaution of parking in a different place to make out his report. He would not tempt fate by stopping across from the Simon Pharmacy as he always did; anyone familiar with his movements at night would know to lie in wait for him there. When he had finished making out his careful statement, Sam put the board down and felt as though something was just about to be pressed against the back of his neck. He flipped the car into gear and drove at an unusually high speed, for him, to the drive-in and the sanctuary of its bright lights.

When he had finished a root-beer float, and topped it off with a piece of lemon pie, he returned to his car and to the city it was his duty to protect. Not till the sky streaked with light and then came aglow did the feeling leave him that he was being silently watched, that at some time he had passed close to danger. At eight in the morning he drove his car with careful skill into the police-department parking lot. This past night, at least, he had earned his pay.

— 7 —

Bill Gillespie waited impatiently while the long-distance operator made the connection. Ordinarily he would have assigned this routine check to someone else, but he had personal reasons for waiting to do it himself. Virgil Tibbs was his alibi now for whatever happened, but he did not want to settle for an alibi—he wanted to catch the killer himself. The hotel clerk came on the line.

"You have an Eric Kaufmann registered with you?" Gillespie asked.

"Yes, sir, we have."

"You understand who I am. Now tell me what you can about Kaufmann's movements night before last. When was he registered, when did he come in, and all that. Spell it out in detail as close as you can. Wait a minute."

Gillespie reached for a block of scratch paper. He started to write "Kaufmann" at the top of the sheet and then stopped in time. Someone might see it. It had been his own idea to check Kaufmann's alibi and he didn't want to tip his hand to anyone. "OK, shoot."

"Mr. Kaufmann registered with us four days ago. He took a moderate-priced room with bath. Night before last, he came in sometime after midnight, actually closer to two, I should say. The night man admits that he cannot fix the time very accurately as he had been dozing up to the time that Mr. Kaufmann came in and didn't look at the clock. He believes it was about two when Mr. Kaufmann went up with him. He does remember that Mr. Kaufmann remarked to him that he had taken a meal before coming to the hotel and was afraid he had been unwise in eating cherry pie at that hour."

Gillespie interrupted. "How does it happen that you have all of this information so conveniently at hand? Were you expecting my call?"

"No, sir, actually I talked to the night man at the request of one of your men yesterday when he phoned me—Mr. Tibbs I believe he said his name was."

The chief grunted into the telephone. "Uh...OK, and thanks. Mention this call to no one, of course."

"Certainly not, sir; Mr. Tibbs warned us about that. But we knew anyway. I hope you get your man; I'm sure you will."

"Thank you," Gillespie concluded, and hung up.

He told himself as he leaned back in his chair that he had no reasonable grounds for getting sore. He had told Virgil to investigate the murder and Virgil was following his orders. Which was what he had better do. Anyhow, Kaufmann was in the clear. At that moment Arnold poked his head in the door.

"Chief, Ralph, the night man at the drive-in, just phoned. He stayed over to eat his breakfast before he went home. He says a man is at the diner, just drove up through town, and Ralph thinks he knows something about the murder."

"Any car description?" Gillespie snapped.

"Pink Pontiac, this year's. California license."

"Go get him," Gillespie ordered. "Ask him politely to see me for a few minutes. And bring Ralph in here as quick as you can."

Gillespie leaned back and thought for a while. Ralph

73

was none too reliable, but he might have something. Ralph's mind was limited, but at times he had a glint of intelligence, the instinct of an animal for its enemies. To Ralph anything that upset the status quo would be an enemy. Asking a passing motorist for his cooperation wasn't out of line even if the counterman was imagining things. The pressure of the case was making Gillespie jittery. He had consulted with himself about it and had decided to control his temper a little better, at least until the case was over. He was still new on the job and a blunder could cost him his whole future career. He knew that he was capable of blundering if he didn't take the time to watch his steps.

Virgil Tibbs appeared at the door of his office. At that precise moment Bill did not want to see the Negro detective—as a matter of fact he did not want to see him at any time—but he recognized necessity when it stood before him.

"Morning, Virgil," he said lazily. "Making any progress on the case?"

Tibbs nodded. "Yes, I believe I am."

Gillespie bristled with suspicion. "Tell me about it," he ordered.

"I'll be glad to, Chief Gillespie, as soon as I'm able. What I have now isn't pinned down tight enough to bring it to your attention. As soon as it is, I'll report to you in full."

Stalling, Gillespie thought to himself. *Won't admit it*. He let the matter drop. Arnold put his head in the door.

"Mr. Gottschalk is here to see you, Chief."

"Gottschalk?"

"The gentleman with the pink California Pontiac."

"Oh. Ask him to come in."

Gottschalk appeared in the doorway before Virgil Tibbs could leave. He was a middle-aged man and

74

portly, with a crew haircut and a capable air. "Am I in trouble?" he asked abruptly.

Bill Gillespie waved him to a chair. "I don't think so, Mr. Gottschalk. But I would appreciate it if you could spare me a little of your time. We had a murder here a couple of nights ago and we thought you might possibly shed some light on it for us."

As soon as Gillespie finished speaking, Virgil Tibbs turned around in the doorway, came back into the office, and sat down. Gillespie noted it, but did not comment.

"Your name *is* Gottschalk, I believe?" Gillespie asked. It was clearly an invitation to supply additional information. Gottschalk reached into his breast pocket, removed his wallet, and laid a business card on Gillespie's desk.

"May I have one?" Tibbs requested.

"Oh, certainly." Gottschalk handed over the card. "You are...ah...on the force?"

"My name is Virgil Tibbs. I'm investigating the murder Chief Gillespie mentioned."

"Excuse me, I didn't understand." Gottschalk held out his hand. The two men shook hands without rising. Then Tibbs sat back quietly, waiting for Gillespie to go on. Arnold appeared again in the doorway. "Ralph is here," he said tersely. Gillespie hesitated, started to rise as if to leave the room. Just then Ralph appeared in the doorway, looked at Gottschalk, and pointed dramatically. "That's him," he declared.

Gillespie sat down again. Gottschalk craned his neck to look at Ralph and then turned back, frankly bewildered. Arnold remained in the doorway, hesitant as to what to do.

"What about this gentleman, Ralph?" Gillespie asked easily.

The counterman took a deep breath. "Well, I forgot

all about it until he showed up again, but this fellow, I mean him there, was in the diner the night of the murder, 'bout forty-five minutes before Mr. Wood came in."

"I don't understand any of this," Gottschalk said.

"Before he came in I was mopping up the front of the place," Ralph went on, "so I would have seen any other cars that went by. His was the only one."

"Did you notice which direction he came from?" Gillespie asked.

"Yeah, he was goin' south."

"Go on."

"Well, I found out later that Sam—I mean Mr. Wood—found the body of the Italian fellow right in the middle of the highway. No other car went through after this fellow did until Mr. Wood found the body." Ralph paused and gulped. "So I figure he done it."

Gottschalk sprang out of his chair with astonishing speed for a man of his bulk. Then he sensibly sat down again.

Bill Gillespie had an inspiration. "It's all yours, Virgil," he said, and leaned back. The idea of having a whipping boy available who could take none of the credit, but all of the blame in the event of a misfire was beginning to appeal to him. And while he did not like to admit it to himself, he knew that Tibbs had something on the ball. How much he was not yet prepared to estimate, but the unhappy suspicion lurked that Tibbs might be better than anyone on the local force, which included himself. Gillespie felt much as a student pilot does who is sure he knows how to fly but who, faced with an unexpected situation which he has never before been called upon to meet, dearly wishes to have his instructor take over the responsibility. Gillespie had never had an instructor on whom to rely, which made it just a little bit worse.

"I see by your card, Mr. Gottschalk," Tibbs began, "that you are a field-test engineer."

"That's right," Gottschalk replied in a reasonable tone of voice. "We've heavily tied in with the work at the Cape. I was on my way down there when I passed through here."

"To be at the shoot they had yesterday?"

"Yes, that's right, Mr. Tibbs."

"What's the Cape?" Gillespie interjected.

"Cape Kennedy."

"Oh, of course." Gillespie nodded to Tibbs to go on. Then he glanced over at Ralph. The counterman was standing with his mouth partway open, as though struck by the fact that the man at whom he had pointed the finger of suspicion had something to do with the spectacular events about which he had read in the papers.

"After you stopped at the diner, Mr. Gottschalk, did you continue on south through the city?"

"Yes, I did. I stayed right on the highway. In fact I didn't stop until I needed gas about a hundred and fifty miles or so down the line."

"What is your security clearance, Mr. Gottschalk?" Tibbs asked.

"Secret and Q."

"Then you have done, or are doing, nuclear work."

"Yes, that's right. Our company has several contracts in the field."

"To clear up a point, may I ask why you were driving at that hour instead of flying down or possibly taking the train?"

"That's a reasonable question, Mr. Tibbs. I drove down this time because I hoped to have my wife join me and we would take a week on the Keys after the shoot. That is, if it went well. I can only say generally that after the shoot it was necessary for me to go back to the plant, which is why I am here now."

77

"In other words, you drove down so you would have your car available in case Mrs. Gottschalk could join you for a week's vacation?"

"Exactly."

"And the reason for driving that late?"

"The heat. It was fierce. I don't have air-conditioning in the car, so I chose to drive at night, at least as much as I safely could, in order to be a little more comfortable."

"Then the only thing left to ask you, sir, is whether or not, in driving through Wells, you noticed anything unusual in any way. I'm assuming you didn't see a body in the road or you would have stopped. But did you see anything else that might be helpful? Any pedestrians? Any signs of any sort of activity?"

Gottschalk shook his head. "I'm not trying to hold out on you to avoid involvement, but I truthfully didn't see anything at all. In fact, if you will excuse my saying so, the town appeared completely dead to me."

Tibbs rose. "You have been very helpful, sir, and we appreciate your willingness to take the time on our behalf."

Gottschalk swung to his feet. "Am I free to go now?"

"Of course, sir. Technically you were free to go at any time and did not need to come here. I hope it was made clear to you that this was strictly a request."

"Frankly," Gottschalk replied, "that wasn't the impression I got. I thought I had fallen into one of those local speed traps or trick-ordinance gimmicks that you hear about. I fully expected to have to pay a fine."

"Chief Gillespie and the other responsible leaders of this city don't do things like that. Let me say officially that you are not under suspicion in any way."

"That's a relief; I wish all cops were like you. And if I may say so without offense, I'm glad to see that democracy has hit the south in something besides the political sense. Good-bye, gentlemen."

The office cleared, but Gillespie motioned to Tibbs to remain. He did not invite him to sit down again, so Tibbs stood waiting until the others were well out of range. Then Gillespie picked up a pencil and began to roll it between his fingers. "Virgil, I let you go ahead with the interview since you are supposed to be handling this case, but do you think it was the smart thing to tell that man that he was officially clear of any suspicion? He works for a very important company. If he reports that back to them, and he might do just that, then what are you going to do if you find out he knows more than he told us just now?" Gillespie leaned back in his chair. "Consider this if you haven't already. This man drove south through town, by his own admission right past the place where Sam found the body—I mean where Mr. Wood found the body. And no other car was seen to go either way after that. Sure he doesn't *look* guilty on the face of it, but he was at the scene of the crime at approximately the time of the crime. You remember, don't you, what the doctor said about the time of Mantoli's death. He fixed the time at just about the very moment that your friend Gottschalk was driving through. And you told him he was officially cleared of all suspicion."

If Tibbs was ruffled, he failed to show it. "Those are very reasonable points you raised, Chief Gillespie, and I would agree with you completely except for one thing."

"And what's that, Virgil?"

"The fact that Mantoli wasn't killed where his body was found."

79

— 8 —

At four o'clock that afternoon, Sam Wood checked in at the station to see what was up. He caught a knowing look from Pete, now on day duty, as he walked in the door, so Sam headed for the washroom and in a few moments Pete joined him.

"Your friend Virgil put Gillespie over the barrel for good this morning," Pete confided.

Sam bent over and made sure that the small toilet cubicles were empty. "What happened?" he asked.

"As near as I can get it, Gillespie dug up another suspect and Virgil sent him down the chute, too."

"Another suspect?" Sam inquired.

"Yeah; some guy who was driving through that night just as the murder was taking place. Ralph, the kid out at the diner, spotted him and Gillespie had him brought in. Then he turned it over to Virgil and Virgil let him loose."

"And Gillespie let him get away with it?"

"Yep. Virgil and Gillespie had a little talk afterward...."

"I'll bet they did."

"No, you don't get me—a real nice *friendly* talk. Virgil told Gillespie something; when Arnold went past the door, there was Gillespie, as meek as Moses, listening to Virgil explain it to him. Arnold didn't get the

80

drift, but it must have been something good."

"Maybe we could ask Virgil about it. Ask him if there are any developments. Show interest in his work."

"Is he here?"

"No, he's been out all day. Took that old car he's got and left. No one knows where he is."

"Maybe he got lonesome and went down to find some nice black girl to shack up with him." As soon as he had uttered the words, Sam was ashamed of himself. He wished he hadn't said them.

"I don't know," Pete answered slowly. "He's awful smart for a black boy. I bet he's working on the case somehow."

Sam made amends, and was glad he could. "I was just kiddin'. Virgil's all right. It wouldn't fool me if he came out on top on this thing."

"If he does, Gillespie'll take it away from him."

"Well, anyway, he's no dope."

"Smartest black I ever saw," Pete concluded; then he added a remarkable tribute. "He oughta been a white man."

Sam nodded his agreement.

Reverend Amos Whiteburn, despite the heat of the day and the presumed informality of his own home, wore clerical black. The parlor was poor and dingy; what furniture there was had not been new for decades. The cheap rug was threadbare and the window curtains totally disillusioned. Nevertheless the tiny room was clean and was as presentable as its furnishings would permit.

"As long as I have been in this community," Reverend Whiteburn said in a commanding bass voice, "this is the first time that I have ever been consulted by the police. I take it as an honor."

"Perhaps," Virgil Tibbs suggested, "your spiritual leadership has been such that there has never been any need."

"Extremely kind of you, Mr. Tibbs, but I'm afraid I know to the contrary. Have you spent much time in the South?"

"No more than I have to," Tibbs admitted. "My mother lives here. I'm trying to persuade her to move to California, where I can give her a better home, but she is elderly and has other children on the East Coast."

"I understand," the minister agreed, his big voice almost booming in the little room. "For some of our people who have lived here all of their lives, the shock of entering a different climate of opinion would be considerable."

Tibbs went on: "Two nights ago, a man was murdered here; you must know about it. I'm investigating that murder—with official approval. Right now I want to discover two things: the place where the murder was done and, if I can, the weapon used."

Reverend Whiteburn leaned forward so that his chair strained under his bulk. "It was my understanding that the poor man met his fate in the middle of the highway."

"He didn't," Tibbs replied.

The minister rubbed his big chin. "Are you at liberty to go any further?" he asked.

"This is an official conversation," Tibbs told him, "and is not to be repeated to anyone."

"It will not be," the minister assured him gravely.

"Maestro Mantoli was killed somewhere on the outskirts or in this general area."

The minister shifted once more in his uncomfortable chair. "How did you determine that?" he interrupted.

"By examining the body, plus a reasonable deduction, that's all."

The minister hesitated and then spoke most carefully. "Mr. Tibbs, are any of our people suspect, either directly or indirectly, in this case?"

"To the best of my knowledge," Tibbs answered with equal care, "no one has suggested that the murderer is necessarily a Negro."

"That," the minister replied, "is in itself a small miracle. But I interrupted you; please go on."

Tibbs studied the big man, who looked like a retired heavyweight boxer, and then took the plunge. "Mantoli was killed with a piece of unfinished wood—pine, I think, but I won't know for sure until I hear from the Forest Products Laboratory. I recovered a sliver from the corpse and sent it to them. I want to find that piece of wood. To try to do so alone would be almost impossible. I came to you because I hear that you are very active in Negro youth programs."

The forehead of Reverend Whiteburn corrugated in thought. He put his fingertips together and then bounced them very gently. "If it was used as a club, it would not be too large. It would have to be a fairly short piece of wood."

"Something like that, perhaps two feet long."

"Hmm. That sounds as if it could be a piece of firewood." When he fell silent once more, Tibbs waited patiently. After several seconds the big man spoke again. "You know...how does this sound, Mr. Tibbs: I will tell our young people—I mean the boys and girls who belong to our club for ten- to fifteen-year-olds—that I want to put in a stock of firewood for the church. I will send them out for suitable pieces, but I'll insist that they take nothing from anyone's woodpile, even if it is freely offered. I'll make a game out of it. As they bring in their findings, and they will bring in plenty, I'll try to find what you're looking for, that is if there is any way to tell."

"Some brownish dried blood on the end. It wouldn't look like blood, not to children, anyway. It's a very long chance at the best."

Reverend Whiteburn regarded the problem as solved. "We'll get on this right away. I can't promise results, of course, but we will gather in a good percentage of the loose wood around this area. And the children need never know the real purpose of the project."

"We could use you in California," Tibbs said admiringly.

His host answered him simply. "I'm needed here."

Bill Gillespie picked up his phone when it rang, and barked, "Yes?"

"Bill, if you can get away for a few minutes, I wish you would step over to my office. Several councilmen are here and you ought to be in on this."

Gillespie recognized the mayor's voice without comment. "I'll be right over, Frank," he replied, and hung up. As he passed through the lobby, he gave the desk man a piercing glance and noted with satisfaction a slight flicker of fear in the man's eyes when he looked back. Then he walked out into the bright sunshine, feeling pretty good, and reflected that whatever Frank Schubert had on his mind, he would be able to handle it without trouble.

It wasn't quite that easy. Schubert welcomed him into his office and waved his arm toward the three other men who were waiting. "You know Mr. Dennis, Mr. Shubie, and Mr. Watkins, Bill."

"Certainly. Good afternoon, gentlemen." Gillespie

sat down with the air of a highly placed executive who has been called upon to testify. At least that was the effect he tried for. And he intended to remain quiet and courteous no matter what lay ahead, for the four men facing him had enough votes on the Council to oust him from his job.

"Bill, the boys asked me to invite you over to discuss the Mantoli murder. Naturally we're all quite concerned about it."

Watkins interrupted. "Coming to the point, Mr. Gillespie, we want to know what's being done and also what's going on."

"Isn't that the same question?" Gillespie asked.

"I mean we want to know what's being done to clear up the murder and what all the rumors are about you having a nigger cop in the station."

Gillespie straightened his shoulders. "I'll take your questions in reverse order, Mr. Watkins. One of our men rushed ahead too fast and picked up a black boy in the station. He had a lot of money on him and so my man ran him in."

"Right thing to do," Watkins clipped.

"When I questioned him, he said he was a cop out in California. I checked up, of course, and he was."

"This isn't California," Shubie contributed.

"I know that," Gillespie snapped, and then checked himself quickly. "I'm sorry, just thinking about him makes me mad." He looked at Shubie and saw that the explanation was satisfactory. "Anyway, George Endicott stuck in his oar. I don't mean to be disrespectful to a councilman, but I don't think he knows how to run a police department. Well, Mr. Endicott got hold of the chief of police that this black boy Virgil works for and found out that Virgil was a homicide specialist. So he up and borrowed him to help us out here."

"That's this nigger," Watkins said.

"That's the one," Gillespie agreed. "Without passing the buck, Mr. Schubert told me to use him and he's the boss; I did what he asked me to."

"Well, I don't like it," Watkins exclaimed, and half rose to his feet. "I don't want no nigger running around this town asking questions of white people like he thought he was somebody. He wanted to talk to my night man, Ralph, at the diner, but Ralph wouldn't let him in. And he was down at the bank acting like he was a white man. A few of the boys are getting ready to teach him his place, and they will, too, if you don't get him out of here."

Gillespie looked at Frank Schubert and waited for the mayor to pick up the ball. When he found he was the center of attention, Schubert reached into his desk and produced a small bundle of newspapers. "Mantoli wasn't so much of a big shot, but when he got himself murdered it made news. It made more news when a colored cop came on the job. If you haven't seen all of these, you better take a look. You know we're getting a lot of press attention. So far it's all been to the good and a lot of free publicity for the music festival."

Dennis spoke for the first time. "Horse shit," he said.

Schubert looked at him as if he was trying to be patient but was finding it an increasingly hard job. "Luke, I know you've been against the music-festival idea all along and that's your right. But like it or not, we're stuck with it now and we've got to go through with it. If it flops, you were right, no argument about it. If it goes over, then maybe it will pump some money into this town and we'll all make out."

"Maybe," Dennis amended.

Schubert turned back to the newspapers. "Gentlemen, I got a phone call from *Newsweek* a few minutes before you came here. They wanted a full rundown on our use of Tibbs. If they run it, that means national publicity for all of us."

"And what the hell will our own people think?" Watkins demanded.

"Will, it doesn't make any difference. We're stuck with this nigger now until we can dump him or until Bill here cleans up the case." Schubert turned toward Gillespie. "That's what I wanted to ask you about. I'm not trying to put turpentine on your tail, but are you going to get us out of this fairly soon?"

Gillespie put a bite into his voice as he answered. "There's a regular routine for this sort of thing, a routine that gets results. We're following it. In addition to that, I'm doing some investigating personally, I don't want to tell you gentlemen definitely when we will have our man under lock and key, but I will tell you, in confidence, that we are getting results. Furthermore I'm keeping Virgil under control and if he gets one bit out of line in this town, I'll slap him down hard. I know he was down at the bank, but he was very respectful there and so far he hasn't done anything that I can pin him for."

"I still don't like it," Watkins insisted. "No news magazine in New York run by a bunch of nigger lovers is going to tell us what to do in our town. We live here and we run this place."

Frank Schubert slapped the palm of his hand hard against the top of his desk. "Will, we all feel the same way, there's no question about that. But be practical. Gillespie is keeping this buck where he wants him. As for *Newsweek*, I don't know who runs it and frankly I don't care. I like it and I subscribe to it. Now be reasonable. We got to ride it out. And this could be a big break for us."

"I don't care what we do," Watkins retorted. "But I want to get rid of that nigger before the boys get impatient and rough him up. *Then* we'll get some publicity that we don't want. We might even get the FBI down here...."

Schubert hit the desk again. "Sure, sure. But the point is, we all want to get the case over with and get rid of the shine boy. Bill here says he has things under control. If he says so, then that's it." He turned to Gillespie. "We're with you, Bill, you know that. Go ahead and do your job; just don't let it drag on too long. When that's done, everything will be solved and maybe we can get back to normal around here."

Dennis turned it sour. "No, we can't; first we've got to have our damn music festival and keep our women locked up nights while the tourists are in town. We're in some shape: we've got nice logs for the people to sit on and a stiff for a conductor. After we clean up that mess, then maybe we can get back to normal business around here."

Schubert teetered on the brink of an explosion but managed to control himself. "This isn't getting us anywhere. I think we all understand each other," he said firmly, "and Bill has work to do. So have I. Thanks for coming, and we'll keep you informed."

The meeting broke up in silence.

On his way back to his office, Bill Gillespie clenched and unclenched his hands. There *had* to be a routine for murder investigation; he decided to dig it out and put it into effect. He had a staff and he was going to see that they went to work.

When Sam Wood reported for work at a quarter of twelve that night, he was surprised to find Virgil Tibbs sitting quietly in the lobby. He was even more surprised when he learned that Virgil was waiting for him.

After Sam had completed his check-in procedure, Tibbs came over and spoke to him. "If you don't mind,

I'd like to ride with you tonight."

Sam was puzzled by the request. He could think of several reasons why the Negro detective should and should not ride with him. "You mean all night?" Sam asked.

Tibbs nodded. "All night."

"I don't know what Gillespie would say." Sam hesitated.

"He told me to do what I liked. I'd like to ride with you."

"Come along then." Sam didn't like the idea of eight hours of companionship with Tibbs, but then he reflected that after three years of patrolling his shift alone, it wouldn't hurt too much to have a passenger for one night. In fact it might be a good night to have someone else in the car. He recalled with a stab of conscience his uneasy concern of the previous night. And if he had refused to take Tibbs, Gillespie might have lit into him for that, too. The night man was a witness that Tibbs had asked him and had indicated that Gillespie had given his blessing. Sam decided to make the best of it and led the way to his patrol car.

When Sam slid behind the wheel, Tibbs opened the opposite door with quiet casualness and sat in the front seat beside him. Sam gripped the wheel firmly and wondered what to say about it. Still, they had sat this way on the drive up to the Endicott house; very well, he could stand it again. He started the engine and backed out of the police parking lot.

"What do you want me to do?" he asked as soon as the car was well away from the station.

"If it's not too much trouble," Tibbs replied, "I'd like you, as closely as you can, to do exactly as you did the night Mantoli was killed. Try to follow the same route and at the same speed. Do you think you can do that?"

"I can follow the same route exactly, and I won't miss the time by five minutes when I make out my report."

"That would help a great deal. Do you want me to keep still and just ride?"

"Talk all you like," Sam retorted. "You won't mix me up any."

Nevertheless they rode silently for some time. Sam took a steadily mounting professional pride in being able to guide his car expertly over the very tracks he had taken. He glanced at his watch. "Are you learning anything?" he asked.

"I'm learning how hot it can be in the middle of the night," Tibbs answered.

"I thought you knew that," Sam reminded him.

"Touché," Tibbs replied.

"Exactly what does that word mean?" Sam asked.

"It's a fencing term. When your opponent scores, you acknowledge it by saying 'touché.' Literally it means 'touched.'"

"In what language?"

"French."

"You've got a lot of education, Virgil, I'll grant you that." Sam swung the car silently around a corner and glanced at his watch.

"I can't drive as well as you can," Tibbs replied. "I've never seen a man who was better."

Despite himself Sam was pleased; he knew that if he could do nothing else, he could drive a car with the best. He was glad that someone else was aware of it, too. Despite his training, he was beginning to like Tibbs as a person.

"Maybe you know the answer to something, Virgil. I read a story once about a man that was real scared. He was out walking at night just waiting for somebody to jump out at him and he thought he could smell fear in the air, if that makes sense. Anyhow, the writer used a word for it—I can't remember it, but it began with an *m*. Sort of—oh, cat sounding. I remember I looked it up at the time."

"Hm-m. Let me think. Could it be 'miasma'?" Tibbs said.

"That's it," Sam exclaimed. "That thing has been bothering me. It's kind of a rare word. How come you know it?"

"I read it in a story, too. More than once, so it was impressed on my mind. Just a coincidence."

"I wish I could have gone to school longer," Sam said, astonishing himself with the burst of confidence. "I went to high school for a while and then I got a job in a garage. I worked there for a while before I got this job."

"Did you go through the FBI school?" Tibbs asked.

"No, I didn't, no chance to. Say, that reminds me, I want to ask you something."

Tibbs waited a moment, then he said, "Go ahead and ask."

"Maybe this isn't any of my business but I heard that you told something to Gillespie today that seems to have shook him. I'd sure like to know what it was."

Virgil Tibbs stared out the window for a moment and inspected the pavement over which they were riding. "I told him that Mantoli wasn't killed where you found him, that his body had been brought there and dumped. That was why Gottschalk, the missile engineer, is obviously in the clear. The body undoubtedly wasn't there when he went through. It had to be brought from the scene of the murder to the highway and you found it within minutes."

"Virgil, how the hell do you know all this?"

"You'd know it, too, Sam, if you'd had a chance to examine the body."

Sam winced under the use of his first name. Just when he found himself beginning to like the dark man beside him, he did something to suggest equality and that Sam simply would not allow. But for the moment he decided to let it ride. He asked a question instead; one word was enough: "How?"

"From the palms of the hands."

"Suppose you take it from the top." Still irked, Sam tried to make it sound like a command, but when he formed the words they were in a milder tone.

"All right, Sam, let's go back to the moment that Mantoli was hit on the head. We know now that it was a fatal blow, but it isn't clear whether the man died instantly or was still conscious for at least a few seconds after he was struck."

Sam swung the car up a gentle grade and again glanced at his watch. He was exactly on schedule. And he was listening carefully.

"Now if the man died instantly, or was knocked unconscious at once, exactly what would happen?"

"He would fall down."

"Yes, but *how* would he fall down? Remember now, he's either unconscious or dead."

Sam thought about that one for a moment. "I think he'd go down like a sack of potatoes." He glanced over at Tibbs, who was half turned toward him, his right arm resting on the windowsill.

"That's exactly right; his knees would unlock, his shoulders would sag, his head would fall forward, and down he would go more or less in a heap."

Sam's mind leaped ahead as the light began to dawn. "But Mantoli's body was all spread out. His hands were over his head!"

"That's right," Tibbs agreed. "I saw the pictures of the body just as you found it."

"Wait a minute," Sam interrupted. "Suppose he was

still conscious for a few seconds or so after he was hit...."

"Go on," Tibbs invited.

"Then he'd throw out his arms and try to save himself."

"Now you're beginning to sound like a homicide man," Virgil encouraged.

"And that's the way I found him."

"That's right."

"So perhaps he was conscious after he was hit."

Sam was so interested in the conversation that he missed a turning. Looking quickly behind him, he made a U turn a quarter of the way up the block and fed a spurt of gas to make up the time he had lost.

"I don't think so," Tibbs said.

"Maybe I missed a point."

"Suppose Mantoli had been hit where you found him. For his body to be spread out that way, he would have had to try and break his fall with his hands."

"I get it!" Sam exploded. "If he had done that, the pavement would have scratched his hands, probably taken off some skin."

"So?"

"Then if there was no skin off the palms of the hands, or any marks like that, that wasn't where he fell."

"Or if it was," Tibbs finished, "someone was careful to spread the body out afterward."

"Yes; though that isn't likely," Sam added. "Because it was in the middle of the highway and a car could have come along any time. I could have."

"Sam," Tibbs said, "you have the makings of a real professional."

This time Sam didn't even notice that Tibbs had used his first name. His mind was jumping ahead to himself, Sam Wood, professional homicide detective. Then he remembered that the black man seated beside him was just that. "How did you learn your trade, Virgil?" he asked.

"Some of the best training in the world and ten years' experience. Everybody who joins the Pasadena force starts out by going to school. It's amazing how much they teach you in a comparatively short time."

Sam thought carefully for a minute before he asked his next question. "Virgil, I'm going to ask you something you aren't going to like. But I want to know. How did they happen to take you? No, that isn't what I mean. I want to ask you point-blank how come a colored man got all those advantages. Now if you want to get mad, go ahead."

Tibbs countered with a question of his own. "You've always lived in the South, haven't you?"

"I've never been further than Atlanta," Sam acknowledged.

"Then it may be hard for you to believe, but there are places in this country where a colored man, to use your words for it, is simply a human being like everybody else. Not everybody feels that way, but enough do so that at home I can go weeks at a time without anybody reminding me that I'm a Negro. Here I can't go fifteen minutes. If you went somewhere where people despised you because of your southern accent, and all you were doing was speaking naturally and the best way that you could, you might have a very slight idea of what it is to be constantly cursed for something that isn't your fault and shouldn't make any difference anyhow."

Sam shook his head. "Some guys down here would kill you for saying a thing like that," he cautioned.

"You made my point," Tibbs replied.

Sam pondered that one for some time. Then he decided that he had had enough conversation and he remained silent until he at last slid the car up to the curb across from the Simon Pharmacy. When he checked his watch for the last time, he was exactly a minute ahead of schedule. Carefully he picked up the clipboard and slowly filled in the report line. Then he looked at his watch, which now showed him that he had succeeded in filling half of the surplus minute. With a clear conscience, he noted down the time and then, switching on the dome light, handed the board silently to Tibbs.

The Negro detective studied it carefully and then handed it back. Sam knew without asking that he would have noticed that the times this evening and on the fatal night were identical. And he was right. "That's amazing, Sam," Tibbs told him. "I know very few men who could have done that and come out right on the nose the way you did." Tibbs paused for a moment. "The next part is the most critical; you know that, of course."

"Naturally I know it, *Mr.* Tibbs." Sam let a touch of venom drip into his voice.

"Then my confidence in you is justified," Tibbs answered. The answer baffled Sam; he wasn't sure just how it was meant. But there was no clear way he could take exception. "All right, let's go," he said, and put the car into gear.

Still edgy, he bumped across the railroad tracks and into shantyville and the Negro area of the city. When he got there, he leaned up over the wheel and watched as usual for sleeping dogs in the street. There were none. Carefully he retraced his route past the tiny, unpainted frame houses, across the siding, and up the street that led past the Purdy house.

At that moment Sam thought about Delores. What if she were to be up and about again? It had happened twice before. That would give a Negro a look at a pretty white girl with no clothes on. Two blocks short of the

Purdy house, Sam swung the car to the right and jogged two blocks down. A small sense of guilt fought for recognition, but Sam suppressed it. And the slight deviation, he felt, was absolutely undetectable.

At the end of the two blocks, Sam turned again to the left and continued up the dark street exactly as he had driven all evening. When the car jolted suddenly on an unpaved patch of road, Sam was startled, then he remembered that at the next corner there was a cross street that would get him back on his route. And it was the block past the Purdy house. When the corner came he took it smoothly, climbed back onto the pavement, and kept straight ahead until he reached the highway. He made his stop, as he always did, and then turned right toward the diner.

As he picked up speed, he wondered what to do with Virgil while he was at the diner; colored were not allowed inside. No clear answer had come to him by the time he pulled into the parking lot. He looked at his watch. "Still on schedule?" Tibbs asked.

Sam nodded. "I stop here fifteen minutes to eat."

Before he could say more, Tibbs relieved his embarrassment. "Go ahead, and don't hurry," he said. "I'll wait for you here."

Inside the diner, Sam's conscience nibbled at his mood. It had been awakened by the slight detour, unimportant in itself and taken for a good reason, but keeping a man waiting, even a black one, while he refreshed himself in comparative comfort annoyed Sam. He turned to Ralph. "Fix me up a ham sandwich to go, and wrap up a piece of pie. Better add a carton of milk and some straws."

"It ain't for that nigger cop, is it?" Ralph demanded. "If it is, we're all out."

Sam pulled himself up to his full height. "When I tell you what to do," he barked, "you do it. What I want

96

that food for is none of your damn business."

Ralph shrank visibly before his eyes, but he did not give up. "My boss won't like it," he countered.

"Move," Sam ordered.

Ralph moved, and balefully. When Sam laid a dollar on the counter, the night man rang it up and handed out the change as though it were something unclean. And when the policeman had closed the door behind him, the thin, pimply youth let a sneer twist his features. "Nigger lover!" No matter what happened now, he was going to tell his boss. *He* was a councilman and Sam Wood wouldn't push *him* around!

Ralph's displeasure didn't faze Sam a bit; it even helped to mollify his conscience. As he passed the food to Virgil Tibbs he felt proud of himself. He started the car, drove down the highway, checked his watch, and received his reward—he was on time to the minute. Carefully he pulled the car up to the spot where he had found the body, turned on his red warning lights, and stopped.

"How closely on time are you?" Tibbs asked.

"To the minute," Sam answered.

"Thank you very much," Tibbs said. "You've helped me a great deal, more than you may realize. And thank you, too, for getting some lunch for me." He paused to take a bite of his sandwich and a sip from the container of milk.

"Now I want to ask you just one thing: Why did you deliberately change your route when we were across the tracks a little while ago?"

— 9 —

When Bill Gillespie was notified that he had been selected as chief of police for the little city of Wells, he had celebrated by buying several books on police administration and the investigation of crime. During his first weeks in Wells they gave him a certain sense of importance despite the fact that he found no time to read them. After his session in Mayor Schubert's office, he decided to crack them without delay. In the quiet of the early evening, after he had eaten well and put on his slippers, he sat down under a good light and made an earnest attempt to study.

He began with Snyder's *Homicide Investigation*. Before he had gone very far he began to appreciate the number of things he did not know, the number of things that he should have done and hadn't. There was the matter of the body, for instance; in place of the careful examination that he should have made, or had made for him, he had taken only a quick look and then had quickly left. Furthermore he had done it before witnesses. Fortunately the witnesses were probably not aware of his deficiency.

Then he remembered that Virgil Tibbs had been there. Not only that, but when invited to do so, Tibbs had made what had apparently been a very thorough examination of the body even though at the time his interest had been purely academic.

Gillespie put the book down and folded his hands behind his head. In a rare mood of fairness, he admitted to himself that it was score one for the Negro detective. Then the happy thought hit him that he could still ask Tibbs for a report on his findings and thus fill the gap in his own investigations. The only thing against it was that it acknowledged Tibbs had some visible ability in his profession. Gillespie weighed the matter for a moment and then decided the price was not too high to pay. He would look better if he asked for the report. He would do so in the morning.

When he finally went to bed, he felt that the evening had been very profitable, and he slept well.

A vestige of his sense of well-being remained in the morning; he planned a number of things he was going to do while he shaved and breakfasted. When he arrived at his office, Eric Kaufmann was waiting to see him. Gillespie received him and waved him to a chair. "What can I do for you?" he asked.

"I want to request a permit to carry a gun," Kaufmann replied, coming right to the point.

"A gun? Why? Do you usually carry large sums of money?" Gillespie asked.

"I wish I were in a position to," Kaufmann answered. "Maestro Mantoli often did and—but I'm not accustomed to."

"Then why *do* you want to carry a gun?"

Kaufmann leaned forward. "I don't want to cast any reflections on your department, Chief Gillespie, and please don't take it that way, but there is a murderer loose in this area. He killed the Maestro. His daughter or I may be next. Until we know why the crime was committed, at least, I will feel a lot better with some protection."

"You are planning to stay here for a while, then?"

"Yes, Mr. Endicott and the committee have asked

99

me to carry on as administrator of the festival activities, at least until someone else can be chosen. Duena— that's Miss Mantoli—is going to stay on until after the concerts as the house guest of the Endicotts. She really has no place else to go."

"I thought she would be going back to Italy with her father's body."

"She'll accompany the body to Italy but she'll be back almost immediately. After all, she was born in this country. Mantoli was an American citizen even though all of his people still live in the old country."

Gillespie was satisfied. "Mr. Kaufmann, have you ever been convicted of a criminal offense?"

Kaufmann reacted. "Certainly not. I've never been in any kind of trouble, not even any serious traffic tickets."

Gillespie spoke into his intercom. "Arnold, will you please take Mr. Kaufmann's application for a gun permit and make up his fingerprint card."

"Thank you very much," Kaufmann said. "Does that mean I may go and buy a gun now?"

"Technically no," Gillespie replied. "The forms have to clear through channels first."

"How long will that take?"

"Oh, a few days. However, if you feel yourself to be in any danger, though I am sure we can give you adequate protection here, go get a gun and bring it back here so we can register it. Then I will give you permission to carry it here in the city until your formal permit comes through. But if you go to Atlanta, or any place like that, please don't take it with you."

Kaufmann stood up. "You've been very kind," he said.

"Not at all." Gillespie rose, shook hands, and settled back in his chair as Kaufmann disappeared.

A moment later, Pete, the desk man, came in with

the daily report. "Anything on it?" Gillespie asked.

Pete shook his head. "Hardly anything; nothing I can see that will help with the Mantoli case." Pete hesitated for a minute. "Did you know that Sam Wood had company part of the time last night?"

Gillespie used his eyebrows for question marks.

"Virgil was with him," Pete explained. "He walked in here a few minutes before midnight and asked to ride along. You had given orders that Virgil was to get cooperation, so Sam took him."

"I bet Sam liked that," Gillespie commented.

"I gather he didn't particularly," Pete replied. "I hear Sam came back in here about four and got rid of him. I hear Sam was mad."

"Where is Virgil now?"

"I don't rightly know. He borrowed a real-estate map of the city, one with all the details and distances on it, and then took off in that car you let him have."

"When he checks in, tell him I want to see him," Gillespie instructed.

"Yes, sir. By the way, there's a letter in that pile on your desk we didn't open. It's marked 'Very Personal.'"

"Thanks." Gillespie nodded his dismissal and fished for the letter in the neat pile that had been placed for him on his desk. When he found it, and saw it was in a plain envelope without return address, he knew what to expect. He tore the envelope open angrily and read, as rapidly as he could to get it over with, the single sheet that it contained:

Gillespie:

Maybe you have wondered why you got the job here when a lot better men who would have taken the job were turned down. It's because you come from the South and we figured you were big enough to keep the niggers in their place. We

101

don't want integration, we want you to keep the damn niggers out of our schools and every other place the nigger lovers want them to get. We don't want them neither in our police department. So get rid of that shine you got working for you and kick him out of town or else. If you don't we'll do it for you and we ain't kidding. If you don't we'll run you out too and your not too big to be put in your place either.

You have been warned.

The rage which Gillespie knew was his greatest problem surged up within him until it was difficult for him to control himself. He knew he should study the letter for a clue to the sender, but he also knew he would not find it. He crumpled the paper into a tight ball in his huge hand and flung it savagely into the wastebasket. They would put him in *his* place, would they! Devoutly he hoped they would try. He clenched his fists and held them up where he could look at them. No southern white trash was going to tell a Texan what to do. And whether they liked it or not, he *was* chief of police and they weren't going to take that away from him. He had not calmed down when the intercom came on.

"Well?" Gillespie demanded.

"Virgil just phoned in to ask what garage took care of our official cars. I told him you wanted to see him. He's coming right in."

The chief's first reaction was rage at the Negro detective who had put him in this position. Then his mood weathervaned in a new direction. He had been *ordered* to get rid of Tibbs. Simply because of that, he resolved to keep him around as long as it pleased him to do so.

He was still framing countermeasures in his mind when there was a tap on his door. He looked up to see the cause of his trouble standing respectfully in the doorway. "You wished to see me, sir?" Tibbs asked.

Gillespie made a conscious effort to speak without strain showing in his voice, and to control his temper. "Yes, Virgil. I've been wondering when you were going to give me a report on your examination of Mantoli's body."

Tibbs's usually expressionless face lit up with distinct surprise. "I gave it to Mr. Arnold two days ago; I thought you had it."

Gillespie covered. "It's probably here on my desk, then. Also I wanted to ask you why you went riding with Sam—I mean Mr. Wood—last night."

"Because I want to know exactly where he was prior to the time he discovered the body. Which streets he drove and when."

"Oh? You considered that important?"

"Yes, sir, I did."

"I see. And did you find out everything you wanted to know?"

"Very nearly. I think I got the rest of it this morning."

"Virgil, I understand Sam dropped you off here last night and that he was sore when he did it. What did you do that upset Mr. Wood? He's a pretty reasonable man ordinarily."

Tibbs hesitated and locked his fingers together before he replied. "Mr. Wood and I got on very well, though at one point he misled me a little, and when I commented on it he dropped me off here without ceremony."

"What do you mean, Mr. Wood misled you? Be specific."

"Since you ask me, Chief Gillespie, I asked him to retrace with me the exact route he followed on the murder night. At one point he made a slight deviation."

Gillespie rocked back in his chair. "Virgil, you've

got to understand that Mr. Wood has been patrolling the streets of the city on the graveyard shift for more than three years. He makes it a point to keep changing his route continuously so that no one can predict just where he will be at any specific time. You can't possibly expect him to remember every turning he made on any specific night, even though it was only a night or two ago."

"Thank you, sir," Tibbs said. "Is there anything else you wanted to ask me?"

Gillespie pondered. He tried to find offense in Tibbs's reply, but if there was any, it did not show on the surface. "No, that's all."

As the Negro left the office, the chief slumped in his chair. A sudden idea had occurred to him, which he didn't like at all. But he wondered why he hadn't thought of it before. The idea was a startling one, but it *could* be the answer.

He shut his eyes and visualized someone holding a piece of wood, swinging it through the air in a vicious, utterly merciless blow that would land on and crush the skull of a little Italian. And the man he now saw swinging the crude club and destroying the life of a fellow human being was Sam Wood.

Sam had had the opportunity, there was no doubt of that. For Sam it would have been easy, for anyone else a tremendous risk. If Sam had walked up to the little man even in the small hours of the night, his victim would not have been on his guard, thinking he had nothing to fear from a policeman in uniform. On a sudden hunch Gillespie picked up the telephone, called the bank, and asked to speak to Mr. Jennings.

"I want to ask you something in strict confidence concerning one of our men here," Gillespie began. "Do you know Sam Wood?"

"I know Mr. Wood very well," Jennings replied promptly.

"What I want to know is this," Gillespie said. "Within the last two months or so has there been any unusual activity in his account? Any unusual deposits or withdrawals? Has he had to borrow money?"

"Ordinarily we try to keep information concerning our depositors confidential," Jennings replied, obviously stalling. "In any event, we don't like to give it out over the telephone. You can appreciate why."

Gillespie's temper shortened again. "All right, all right! You are being cautious and I don't blame you, you're doing your job. But you didn't answer my question."

"Let me understand clearly, Mr. Gillespie," Jennings retorted. "Is this an official request for information?"

"You can consider it that."

"Then of course we'll cooperate. If you will come to my office whenever you find it convenient, I will allow you to look at the records."

"Can't you deliver them to me here?"

"If you get a court order for us to do so, we gladly will," Jennings answered evenly. "Otherwise it would be much better if you could call here, since obviously we don't want to let our records out, and we try to avoid making copies whenever possible."

Satisfied that he could do no better, Gillespie hung up. He was annoyed that the conversation had given him no hint one way or the other. Robbery did not appear to be the motive, but Kaufmann had mentioned that Mantoli habitually carried large sums of money on his person. Sam Wood might have killed and robbed him, leaving enough money behind to divert suspicion. That sort of thing had been done before.

Arnold appeared in the doorway; he had a few sheets of paper in his hand. "Virgil says you want to see his report on Mantoli's body."

"Of course I want to see it," Gillespie snapped. "What have you been sitting on it for?"

"I didn't think you wanted it," Arnold replied. He shrugged and left.

Bill Gillespie looked over the report. As he read from paragraph to paragraph, he began to hate the document. He hated it because it was the work of an inferior and at the same time better than he himself could have done or had done. But it would save him from possible serious embarrassment later on the witness stand if it came to that. He also learned a lot about the late Maestro Mantoli which he had not previously known. Try as he would, however, he could not escape being irritated by the fact that the report was the work of a Negro. They had no right to be smart.

The telephone rang.

Frank Schubert was on the line. "Bill, I hate to bother you but my phone has been going like mad all day. Can you tell me any more than you could yesterday about our case? The council is getting very restless and everybody I know in town has been calling up asking when the murderer will be caught."

"Damn it, Frank, I wish you'd tell these people to get out of your hair and mine and let me run this murder investigation. Pressure doesn't help, you ought to know that."

Mayor Schubert hesitated. "All right, Bill. I understand how you feel. Ah...about one other matter, that colored boy from California: did you get rid of him yet?"

"No, and I'm not going to." Gillespie kept his voice under control with an effort.

"I think it would be a good idea, Bill."

"For personal reasons I'll be damned if I will." Gillespie's voice rose in spite of him. "Frank, I've got to go now. I promise you I'll call as soon as I have anything to report."

"Oh. All right, Bill," Schubert said, and hung up. Gillespie realized that the mayor's patience, too, was beginning to wear thin. And if Frank Schubert got too angry, that was the end of the chief-of-police job.

Gillespie flipped a key on the intercom. "Where's Virgil?" he asked.

"He went out," Pete answered. "Got a call from a Reverend Somebody and lit out of here on the double. Do you want him?"

"Later," Gillespie said, and killed the circuit. A dozen different emotions were tearing at him, all pulling in different directions. He got up, clapped on his hat, and headed for his car. One thing was going to be settled anyway; he was off to the bank to see Jennings.

The bank manager received him courteously and sent immediately for Sam Wood's file. Gillespie was pleased to note that his word, and his presence, carried *some* weight in this city he was beginning cordially to dislike. When the file was delivered, Jennings looked it over in silence and then kept it in his hands while he spoke.

"Mr. Wood has had an account with us for several years. It has never been more than a few hundred dollars. Twice he has been overdrawn but covered the checks in question promptly enough to protect his credit standing. Deposits and withdrawals have been consistent for some time."

"Is there any more?" Gillespie asked impatiently.

"I was coming to that," Jennings replied, unruffled. "Two days ago, Mr. Wood came in and paid off the mortgage on his home. It is a small place and not very much was due. He deposited a check which he stated was a legacy he had received in the mail, and a little over six hundred dollars in cash."

"Six hundred dollars in cash!" Gillespie repeated. "That sounds very unusual to me."

"Yes and no," the banker replied. "Many people still hoard their savings in mattresses and cookie jars despite the amount that is lost each year that way."

"But not when they have bank accounts and have had them for several years," Gillespie said. The weight of the evidence that he had just received was beginning to sink in; he had called for a long forward pass and it was just falling securely into his arms on the five-yard line.

Sam Wood made it a point to check in at the station around four o'clock each day. On this particular day he did not want to do so but felt that he should in order to keep up appearances. During the latter part of the night, when he had been alone, he had come to realize the injustice he had done his uninvited companion. He had spent considerable time trying to figure out how his simple deception had been detected. But since it had been, Sam did not want to run into Virgil Tibbs.

When he walked into the lobby, Sam saw Eric Kaufmann talking with Pete at the desk. Kaufmann was displaying a small gun and Pete was apparently taking down the make and serial number.

Kaufmann looked around, saw Sam, and came over to speak to him. "Can you spare me a moment?" Kaufmann asked. "I'll be through here right away."

"Of course." Sam sat down on a bench against the wall, where there was at least a small measure of privacy. In a minute or two Kaufmann slid the little gun into his pocket and came over to sit beside Sam.

"First of all," he began, "I want to square things with you. I'm damn sorry I got hairy with you the other night. I was very worried and upset, but that's still no excuse."

"Forget it," Sam said gallantly.

"When I stopped to think about it, I realized how thoughtful of you it was to drive all the way up to Endicotts' just to look after all of us up there. Duena and I want you to know we appreciate it a great deal."

The last sentence made Sam feel as though he had been solidly hit in the pit of his stomach. For a moment he made no reply.

"When I thought it over," Kaufmann continued, "I came in and got a permit to carry a gun."

"Do you know how to use one?" Sam asked.

"Not very well. But I don't ever want to use it, really. It's enough to have it to point at somebody if I have to. That's all I want it for, until this thing is over. I presume you're making some progress."

"I can't talk about that," Sam replied. He was sure that was a safe answer.

"I understand. And, oh, yes, before I forget it, Duena asked me to thank you for your kindness to her the day her father was killed. She still isn't herself, but she's coming around better than could be expected. If you knew her as I do, you'd know she's a wonderful girl."

"I'm sure she is," Sam said, meaning every word of it. Then he decided he might as well take the plunge. "I'm surprised you haven't married her."

"I want to very much," Kaufmann replied. "I think all might have gone well, but then this dreadful thing happened. When it is all behind us, and we can leave here, then she may come around."

"You should stand a good chance," Sam said, deliberately torturing himself.

"I hope so."

"Well, I sure wish you the best of luck," Sam lied cordially, and held out his hand. He liked Kaufmann better today in spite of everything. It was nice to like people and to have them like you. Sam looked about him to see if Virgil Tibbs might be there.

Pete saw him looking and called him over to the desk. "The boss wants to see you."

"Right away," Sam acknowledged. He turned toward the corridor that led to Gillespie's office. On the way he stepped in the washroom for a moment to smooth his hair and tuck in his shirt. Even though he had little respect for Gillespie, when he walked into his chief's office he wanted to look, and to be, every inch a competent and reliable police officer. He walked the rest of the way down the corridor and knocked respectfully on the closed door.

It was nearly six when Virgil Tibbs drove his borrowed car onto the official parking lot and climbed wearily from the driver's seat. Before closing the door he reached back inside, then he climbed the steps into the lobby.

The early night man on the desk looked up as Tibbs walked in.

"Well?" he asked.

"Is Chief Gillespie still here, by any chance?" Tibbs asked.

"Yes, he's here, but I don't think he wants to be disturbed right now."

"He has someone with him?" Tibbs inquired.

"No, he's alone. But it had better be pretty important if you want to see him now."

"Please tell him that I'm here and I want to see him," Tibbs said.

The night man took ample time to reach over and flip the intercom key. "Virgil's here," he reported. "I told him not to disturb you, but he insists on coming in."

"All right," Gillespie's voice came out.

"Go on in," the night man said, and returned to the paper he had been reading.

Tibbs walked down the corridor and knocked on Gillespie's door.

Gillespie's voice came through the panel. "I said you could come in."

Virgil Tibbs opened the door and walked quietly into Gillespie's office. When he looked at the big man behind the desk, he saw at once that in some manner he had been badly shaken. "Well? What is it that's so important, Virgil?" Gillespie asked. There was no fire in his words. He spoke with the voice of a man who had made a strong and bold move and who was now asking himself if he had done the right thing.

Tibbs laid a piece of wood on Gillespie's desk. It was a rough, round section of a limb about two inches in diameter and twenty-two inches long. Gillespie looked at it without speaking. "What do you want me to do with that?" he asked.

"It's the murder weapon," Tibbs told him.

Gillespie picked up the fatal piece of wood and examined it curiously. There were unmistakable stains at one end which gave grisly proof of what it probably had done. The chief turned it around in his fingers and then sighted down its length to see how straight it was. "How did you find it?" he asked.

"I had some help," Tibbs acknowledged. He waited for further questions.

Gillespie continued to turn the piece of wood in his fingers. When he didn't speak, Tibbs did. "Is something wrong?" he asked.

"I told you once we could run our own business down here, not that I don't appreciate your bringing this in to me. And your report on Mantoli's body was satisfactory. And I'd better tell you—I arrested Man-

111

toli's murderer personally about an hour ago."

Tibbs audibly drew a quick breath. "Can you tell me—" he began.

"Who he is?" Gillespie supplied.

"... whether you got a confession?" Tibbs finished.

"No, I didn't. He protested, of course." Gillespie stopped and picked up the deadly piece of wood once more. "But he did it. I know. He continued to examine the implement in his hands and then hefted it for weight. "What did this tell you, Virgil?" he asked.

"It would be more accurate to say that it confirmed what I already knew, Chief Gillespie."

"Exactly what would that be?"

"Who the murderer is," Tibbs answered.

Gillespie put the piece of wood back on his desk. "Hmm. Well, I beat you to it. And now if you want to see your friend Sam, you'll find him in the first cell down the hall."

Virgil Tibbs looked at Gillespie with wonder and disbelief and then looked out the window a moment while he collected his thoughts. "Sam Wood?" he asked, as though the idea was beyond him.

"That's right," Gillespie answered. "Sam Wood."

Tibbs sank silently into a chair before Gillespie's desk. "Sir," he said finally, with great care, "I know you won't want to hear this, but I must tell you. Mr. Wood is definitely not guilty. You can see the implications toward your career if you don't let him go." He paused and looked very steadily at Gillespie with his deep-brown eyes. "You see, sir, I know it for a fact that you've got the wrong man."

— 10 —

As a boy Bill Gillespie had been, from the first, considerably bigger than his classmates and the other children with whom he associated. Because of this fact he could dictate the terms of the games that were played and impose his will on others who were not physically his equal. To his credit, Gillespie did not use his size to become a bully and he did not deliberately "pick on" those who might have wanted to disagree with him. But his automatic leadership deprived him of an early education in one of the most important accomplishments he could have had—diplomacy. He was aware of this and it bothered him occasionally.

It bothered him mightily the night after he arrested Sam Wood on suspicion of murder. He thrashed about in his bed, turning from side to side and pounding the pillows, which remained completely docile but gave him not the slightest cooperation. He then got up and made himself some coffee. In his mind he kept reliving the scene in his office; no man had ever stood up to him as Sam Wood had and he admired him for it. Gillespie had won, of course, as he always won, but now plaguing doubts began to parade before him until they seemed to be forming ranks like a Roman phalanx. One large contributing factor was Virgil Tibbs's insistence that Sam Wood was innocent. Gillespie did not want to think much of the Negro investigator, as he had made completely clear, but he knew that the man from Pasadena had an impressive record of being right.

Gillespie hoped, and nearly prayed, for one good, solid, concrete piece of evidence to back his judgment. He liked Sam Wood, apart from the fact that he didn't think he was much of a cop, but he detested murderers, and Sam Wood, he was sure, was a murderer.

Only Sam had denied the charge to the limit of his power and then Virgil Tibbs had backed him up. Gillespie went back to bed and slept the uneasy sleep of the guilty. He felt no better in the morning and went to his office wishing, for the first time, he had not accepted the appointment for a job he was not properly qualified to fill.

He could feel the strain in the air as he walked through the lobby. Pete greeted him respectfully as always, but the words were as empty as blown eggshells. Gillespie sat down in a businesslike way behind his desk and began to go through the pile of mail that was waiting for his attention. Even as he read, an idea shaped in his mind: he would check further into the evidence he had and if it could be satisfactorily explained away, he would consider releasing Sam. He knew he wouldn't actually do it without a "break" one way or the other, but it eased his conscience to feel that he was being fair.

Presently he became aware that something was taking place out in the lobby. He heard voices and he thought he caught the mention of his own name. He would have liked to go out to see what was happening, but the dignity of his office required him to wait to be asked.

He didn't wait long. Arnold appeared in the doorway and paused to be recognized.

"Sir," he said, "we're receiving a complaint out here that I think you should hear. I mean I'm sure of it.

114

Shall I bring the people in?"

The chief nodded his agreement. There were confusing footsteps in the corridor and then two people were ushered into his office. The first was a rawboned man with an extremely lean face which had been weathered into a maze of hairline wrinkles. He was dressed in work clothing and stood with his shoulders forward in an attitude of perpetual suspicion. He wore steel-rimmed glasses, which gave his face an added hardness. He held the corners of his mouth tight from force of habit; Gillespie's first reaction to him was that he would be a mean one if he got drunk.

The other person was a girl, in her mid-teens as far as Gillespie could tell. She wore a sweater-and-skirt combination that emphasized the round ripeness of her body. She was slightly overweight, a fact which her flat-heeled shoes emphasized, but there was no mistaking the significance of every part of her body. Her clothes were much too tight and thrust her breasts upward and out in an exaggerated, unavoidable display. Gillespie thought she was headed for trouble if she had not already arrived.

"You Chief Gillespie?" the narrow man asked. The three words were enough to show his lack of schooling and to reassure Gillespie that he was this man's master.

"That's right," Gillespie said. "What's your problem?"

"My name's Purdy; this here is my daughter Delores." Upon being introduced, Delores turned on a wide smile that was clearly designed to be captivating and significant. Gillespie looked back at the father.

"She's been got into trouble, Chief, and that's why we came down here."

"The usual kind of trouble?"

"I mean she's gonna have a baby. That's the kind of trouble I mean."

115

Gillespie turned to the girl. "How old are you, Delores?" he asked.

"Sixteen," she drawled brightly.

Her father laid a hand on her shoulder. "That ain't exactly right. You see, Delores, she was sick for a while and got behind in school. Kids is awful hard on somebody who ain't as far as she ought to be, so we let it out Delores was fifteen when we moved here a year past. Actually she was seventeen then, so that makes her just eighteen now."

"That makes a lot of difference," Gillespie explained. "In this state if a girl of sixteen gets in a family way, that's statutory rape even though she gives her consent."

"Unless she's married," Purdy put in.

"That's right, unless she's married. But if she's eighteen or over, and gives her consent, then it's fornication, which is a lot less serious offense."

Purdy's face grew harder still. He looked as though he were listening for some sound he expected to hear in the far distance. "Well, what is it if some guy takes an innocent girl like my Delores here and smooth-talks her into doing what she hadn't oughter. Ain't that rape?"

Gillespie shook his head. "That's seduction, and while it's a serious offense, it isn't as bad as rape. Rape belongs with murder, armed robbery, and other offenses that are the most serious in the book. Suppose you both sit down and tell me just what happened."

Taking the cue, Arnold disappeared from the doorway. While Purdy and his daughter were still seating themselves, the intercom buzzed. Bill flipped the switch. "Virgil's in the lobby, Chief. He wants to know if he can have your permission to come in. He says it's important to the case he's working on."

Gillespie drew breath to turn the request down flat. Then a sadistic thought hit him; he wondered how

116

Purdy would like to describe his daughter's troubles with a Negro listening in. Purdy had interrupted him with a correction while he had been explaining the law and that Gillespie had not liked. "Let him come in," he said.

Tibbs entered the room as quietly as possible and sat down on the bench as though he were there to await orders to do some job of work.

"Send him out of here," Purdy said. "I ain't gonna talk about this with no nigger in the room."

"If I want him here, he stays," Gillespie stated. "Now go on with your story and forget he's here."

Purdy refused to give up. "Get him out of here first," he demanded.

To Gillespie's surprise, Tibbs rose quietly to his feet and started for the door. Gillespie looked up in anger, and Tibbs spoke quickly. "I forgot something; I'll be right back." When Purdy looked away from him, Tibbs pointed at the intercom. Then he shut the door behind him on his way out.

Since the situation had been resolved without loss of face, Gillespie moved some papers on his desk, opened a drawer and looked inside, and then flipped a switch on his intercom. Then he leaned back in his chair. "All right, we're alone," he said. "Now tell me what you have to say."

"Well, Delores, she's a real good girl, never done nothin' wrong except what kids always do. Then, without me knowing nothing about it, she meets this here guy who's twice as old as she is. He ain't married so he starts trying to go places with my girl here."

"Why didn't you stop it?" Gillespie demanded.

Purdy turned sour. "Mister, I work all night. I ain't got no time to stay home and take care o' the kids or see what they's doin' every minute. Besides, Delores didn't tell me nothing about it until afterwards."

"He was a real nice guy," Delores contributed. "I couldn't see nothing wrong in it. He was real nice to me."

"Come to the point," Gillespie said. "When did it happen?"

"Real late one night. The missis was asleep like she oughta be, when Delores got outa bed to see this guy, and that's when he had her."

Gillespie turned to the girl. "Tell me about it; exactly what happened."

Delores did her best to look coy; it was a fair imitation. "Well, like Pa said, he was real nice to me. We talked and then we sat real close together and then..." She ran down only from lack of words.

The chief picked up a pencil and tapped it against the desk. "I want you to tell me one thing," he demanded. "Did this man force himself on you so that you had to struggle against him, or did it just work out that he went farther than he should?"

Delores hesitated a long time, long enough to give Gillespie the answer he needed. "I didn't rightly understand everything at the time," she said at length.

Gillespie let his body relax a little. "All right, Delores, this man did you wrong, of course, and we'll arrest him for it. We can charge him with seduction and that's plenty. Now what can you tell me about him?"

Purdy refused to remain silent any longer. "You know him right enough," he exploded. "That's why we wanted to see you personal. It's that night cop you got out supposin' to be protectin' the women all the time. I know his name, too—it's Sam Wood."

When Bill Gillespie was once more alone, he pushed the intercom and gave an order. "Send Virgil in here," he instructed.

"Virgil isn't here," Pete's voice came back.

"Well, where in hell is he?" Gillespie demanded. "I thought he was listening on the intercom."

"Yes, sir, he was. Just as the interview ended, he said something about having been the biggest fool in the country, and beat it."

"Is that all?"

"Yes, sir, except for the fact that he made a very brief phone call on the way out." In that statement Pete lied to his chief. It was not a very serious lie and it was, in fact, Pete thought, an act of mercy. As he had rushed out of the lobby, the Negro detective had paused just a moment to say quickly, "Tell Sam Wood not to worry." Pete required only a fraction of a second to decide not to repeat that remark to Gillespie. It might go hard with the man who did.

The ancient car that Jess the mechanic had loaned to Virgil Tibbs had been designed with adequate but conservative power; consequently it labored somewhat as it steadily pushed its way up the winding curves of the road that led to the Endicott home. When at last it reached the top, the radiator was showing signs of strain. Tibbs parked it on the small level area beside the house, set the brake firmly, and climbed out. A moment later he pressed the bell.

George Endicott opened the door promptly. "Come in, Mr. Tibbs," he invited. He was courteous without being cordial. He led the way to his spectacular living room, sat down, and waved his guest to a seat. "What did you want to see me about?" he asked.

"I want to ask you some questions which I should have thought of long ago," Tibbs replied. "Due to some events which have just taken place down in the city, they are now quite urgent. That's why I asked if I could see you right away."

"All right then," Endicott agreed. "You ask them and

I'll do my best to answer you."

"All right, sir. On the night that Maestro Mantoli was killed, I believe he was up here earlier in the evening; is that right?"

Endicott nodded. "That's right."

"Who was the first person to leave the house?"

"Mr. Kaufmann."

"At about what time did he leave?"

"I should say ten o'clock." Endicott pondered for a moment. "I can't be too exact about that; I don't believe anyone was paying very close attention to the time. We were very much engaged with other things."

"Exactly who was here that evening?"

"There was Enrico—that's Maestro Mantoli—his daughter, Mrs. Endicott and myself, and Mr. Kaufmann."

Virgil Tibbs leaned forward and laced his fingers tightly together. He stared hard at them as he asked the next question. "Can you estimate the time when Maestro Mantoli left here?"

"Eleven, eleven-thirty," Endicott replied.

Tibbs waited a moment. "When he left, how did he get from here down to the city?"

This time Endicott paused before he replied. "I drove him," he said finally.

"Were you two alone?"

"Yes, we were. As soon as we left, the ladies retired."

"Thank you. And about what time did you arrive back here?"

"About an hour after I left. I can't give you the exact time. I told you we were absorbed in other matters that night."

"Where did you drop Maestro Mantoli?"

Endicott showed slight signs of impatience. "I dropped him at his hotel. We had offered to put him up here. He declined because he was a very considerate man and he knew that if he accepted, Mrs. Endicott and I would have had to move out of our room for him. We have a guest room but his daughter was occupying it. So he chose to stay at the hotel despite the fact that it is decidedly second rate."

"From the time you left here together," Tibbs went on, "did you meet anyone else or see anyone else until you returned?"

Endicott stared firmly at his guest. "Mr. Tibbs, I'm not sure I like the tone of that question. Are you asking me to prove an alibi? Are you suggesting that I killed a very close and dear friend?"

Virgil Tibbs pressed his fingers even tighter together. "Mr. Endicott, I'm not implying anything. I am after information, pure and simple. If you saw anyone at that hour when you were down in the city, that could offer a clue as to who might be guilty of the murder."

Endicott stared out of the huge window at the remarkable view which extended for miles over the distant mountains. "All right, I'm sorry," he said. "You have to explore every possibility, of course."

The two men were interrupted when Grace Endicott and Duena Mantoli came into the room. They rose and Tibbs exchanged proper greetings. He noted that the girl seemed to have recovered her composure; her eyes were clear and she looked at him as though she was no longer frightened.

When they were all seated, Grace Endicott asked a question. "Are you making any progress?"

"I believe so, Mrs. Endicott," Tibbs answered, "particularly so today. But progress in any police investigation is a hard thing to define. You may work weeks on something and find it leads up a blind alley. You can never be sure until you have the last piece of evidence you need not only to identify your man, but also to prove his guilt beyond any question of doubt."

"We all appreciate the theory," George Endicott interrupted, "but right now we're more interested in facts. Is there any indication when an arrest will be made?"

Virgil Tibbs studied his fingers. "An arrest has been made," he said, "but it isn't the right man. I know that for a fact."

"Then why is he under arrest?" Endicott demanded.

Tibbs looked up. "Because Chief Gillespie doesn't have sufficient confidence in my opinion to let his prisoner go."

"Who is it?" Grace Endicott asked. "Anyone we know?"

"Yes, you know him, Mrs. Endicott. It's Officer Wood; he was up here with me the last time I called."

Duena Mantoli suddenly sat bolt upright. "Do you mean the fairly big man who was so nice to me the day..."

"That's the man, Miss Mantoli."

"He's accused"—she hesitated and then forced herself to say the words—"of killing my father?"

"That and more," Tibbs replied, "and while no one appears to agree with me at the moment, I am personally sure that he's innocent."

"If that's the case, why don't you prove it?" Endicott asked.

When Tibbs looked up, there was a subdued fire in his eyes. Endicott was startled to see the slender Negro show such a sign of inner vitality. "That is exactly what I am trying to do," he said, "and that is why I am asking you these questions."

Endicott stood up and walked over to the window. There was quiet in the room until he spoke.

"Will Gillespie let you prove it?" he asked, without looking around.

"My job right now," Tibbs answered evenly, "is to protect him from his own mistakes. Sam Wood is one of them. After I do that, I will deliver the person who caused all this to him in such a manner that even he will finally know the truth. Then I'm going home, where I have the right to walk down the sidewalk."

Endicott turned around. "From the time we left here, Mr. Tibbs, I saw no one and I don't believe Maestro Mantoli did, either. That is, up until the time I left him at the door of his hotel. Then I wished him good night and came back here. There is no one, to my knowledge, who can prove what I say, but that is what happened."

"Thank you," Tibbs replied. "Now I want to ask you a very few more questions and I ask that you be particularly careful with the answers. A great deal depends on them. First, I have been told Mr. Mantoli often carried large sums of money. Do you know if he was doing so...the last time you saw him?"

"I have no idea. Actually Enrico did not carry what you would call *large* sums of money. Sometimes he had several hundred dollars on his person, but nothing beyond that, to my knowlege."

"Was he in any way an impulsive person?"

"That's hard to answer," Endicott said.

"I think I can say he was," Duena said unexpectedly. "He sometimes made up his mind on the spur of the minute on things, but he was usually right when he did. If you mean did he have a bad temper, the answer to that is no."

Tibbs addressed his next question to her. "Miss Mantoli, was your father the sort of man who made friends easily?"

"Everyone liked him," Duena replied.

In that grim moment, everyone in the room realized at the same time that there had been one person who did not. But no one voiced the thought.

"One last question," Tibbs said, addressing himself to the girl. "If I had had the honor of meeting your

123

father, do you think he would have liked me?"

The girl lifted her chin and accepted the challenge. "Yes, I am sure of it. I have never known anyone so free of prejudice."

Tibbs rose to his feet. "Thank you. Whether you realize it or not, you have been a great help to me. In a little while I believe you will know why."

"That's good to know," Endicott said.

Then the girl stood up. "I want to go down to the city," she announced. "Perhaps Mr. Tibbs will be kind enough to take me."

"My car is very modest," Tibbs said, "but you are welcome."

"Please wait for me a moment," she requested, and left without further explanation.

When she returned and they stood at the doorway ready to leave, George Endicott rubbed his chin in thought for a moment. "How will you get back?" he asked.

"If I don't get a convenient ride, I'll call you," she promised.

"Do you think you will be safe enough?"

"If I feel I need any help, I'll ask Mr. Tibbs."

Tibbs ushered the girl into his temporary car, climbed in, and started the engine. In the brief time that she had excused herself, she had changed her dress and put on an especially feminine hat. Tibbs thought her quite devastating, but more than that, he sensed she had a firm purpose in mind. There was a set to her jaw, which she did not relax until they were well inside the city.

"Where would you like to go?" Tibbs asked.

"To the police station," she said.

"Are you sure that is a good idea?" he asked her.

"Very sure."

Tibbs drove on without comment until they reached

124

the official parking lot. Then he escorted her up the steps into the lobby. She went straight to the desk. "I would like to see Mr. Wood," she said.

Pete was caught entirely off balance. "Mr. Wood isn't on duty right now," he hedged.

"I know that," Duena Mantoli replied. "He's in jail. I want to see him."

Pete reached for the intercom. "A lady is here to see Sam," he reported. "And Virgil just came in, too."

"Who is she?" Gillespie's voice came out of the box.

"Duena Mantoli," the girl supplied. "You can tell him Mr. Tibbs was kind enough to bring me at my request."

Pete reported over the intercom.

"I'm sorry, she'd better not," Gillespie answered.

"Who was that?" Duena demanded.

"That was Chief Gillespie."

Duena's chin grew very firm once more. "Take me in to see Mr. Gillespie, please," she said. "If he won't see me, I'll call the mayor."

Pete led her down the hall toward Gillespie's office.

Sam Wood had reached the point where his mind had given up and refused, out of pure fatigue, to maintain the extremes of rage, frustration, hopelessness, and bitter disappointment which had racked him during the hours he had been sitting alone. Now he didn't care anymore. He never permitted himself to consider that he might be found guilty, but his career as a police officer was over; he could never return to it now. Shortly before lunchtime, when Gillespie had been out of his office, Arnold had stopped by and brought him up to date. Sam now knew he stood accused of seduction as well as murder. His cup of misfortune and moral exhaustion was brimful.

Sam sat, his forearms resting on his knees, his head

down. It was not a position of shame or defeat; he was simply bone tired. He had exhausted himself thinking and trying to control the impulses which attempted, one after the other, to take command of his mind and body. Pete came and stood beside the bars. "You've got a visitor," he announced.

"My lawyer?" Sam asked.

"He's still out of town, expected back this evening. This is a different visitor." Pete fitted the key and swung the door halfway open. Sam watched him, mildly curious, then his heart gave a great leap. Duena Mantoli walked through the doorway and into the harsh, unyielding jail cell. Profoundly embarrassed, Sam got to his feet. He had not shaved that morning and his shirt collar was undone. He wore no tie. At that moment these things disturbed him more than the accusations which hung over his head.

"Good afternoon, Mr. Wood. Please sit down," Duena said calmly.

Mystified, Sam sat down on the hard board that served as a comfortless bunk. Duena seated herself, straight and graceful, four feet from him. Sam said nothing; he did not trust either his mind or his voice.

"Mr. Wood," Duena said clearly and without emotion, "I have been told that you are accused of killing my father." For a moment her lower lip quivered, then she regained control of herself; very slightly her voice softened in tone and the formality evaporated from her words. "I came here with Mr. Tibbs. He told me that you are not the man who did it."

Sam gripped the edge of the bunk with all the strength of his fingers. His mind, rebelling once more against discipline, told him to turn, to seize this girl, and to hold her tight. So he hung on and wondered if he was supposed to say anything.

"I didn't do it," he said, looking at the concrete floor.

"Please tell me about the night you...found my father," Duena said. She looked straight ahead at the hard blocks that formed the wall of the cell. "I want to know all about it."

"Just..." The words would not come to Sam. "I just found him, that's all. I'd been on patrol all night. I stopped at the diner like I always do and then came down the highway. That's when I found him."

Duena continued to look at the uncompromising wall. "Mr. Wood, I think Mr. Tibbs is right. I don't believe you did it, either." Then she turned and looked at him. "When I met you I was still in the first shock of...everything that happens at a time like that. But even then I felt you were a decent man. I think so now."

Sam turned his head to look at her. "Do you mean you really think I'm innocent?"

"I have a way of telling," Duena said, "a very simple test. Will you submit to it?"

A sense of new life began to flow into Sam. His weary mind came back to the alert. And then, in a burst, he felt he was a man again. He turned to face the girl fully. "You name it," he said. "Whatever it is, I'll do it."

"All right, stand up," Duena instructed.

Sam rose to his feet, resisting the desire to tuck in his shirt, wishing he could just have put on a tie. He felt self-conscious and awkward.

Then, to his utter confusion, the girl got up, walked to him, and stood inches away. He felt his heart quicken as some mysterious mechanism within his body released adrenalin into his bloodstream. And for the first time in many years he was suddenly frightened.

"Your first name is Sam, isn't it?" she said. "I want you to call me Duena. Say it."

"Yes, ma'am," Sam answered, wondering. "Duena," Sam repeated obediently.

"Take hold of me, Sam," the girl said. "I want you to hold me close to you."

Sam's mind, which had said *no* so many hundreds of times during the last twenty-four hours, refused to let him obey. When he didn't move, the girl threw her head back. With her right hand she pulled the hat from her head. Then she shook her head quickly and let her dark-brown hair ripple down the back of her neck. "You said you would do it," she challenged, "now do it." As she spoke the last three words, she closed the gap between them and rested her hands on his shoulders.

Without thinking, without caring for anything else, Sam put his arms around the girl before him. In a confused instant he knew she was warm, and yielding, and beautiful. He never wanted to let her go. The bars of the cell vanished in the surge of manhood he felt within himself.

"Look at me," Duena said.

Sam looked. Sam had held girls in his arms before, but nothing in his lifetime had approached the sensation that engulfed him now.

"Now," the girl said, "I want you to look at me and say, 'Duena, I did not kill your father.' Do it," she commanded.

Sam spoke through the lump that crowded his throat. "Duena..." He tried again. "Duena, I didn't kill your father." Sam's arms let go. They fell to his sides, and strong and courageous as he was, he suddenly wanted to cry. The reaction had been too much.

While he stood there, fighting to regain his composure, he felt the pressure of her hands on his shoulders grow stronger. Then they moved and locked behind his neck. "I believe you," she said. And then, before he realized what was happening to him, Sam felt his head being pulled downward, the warmth of Duena's body against his own, and then a cool, electrifying pressure as she pressed her lips against his.

She was herself again before he could move. Quite calmly she picked her hat up off the floor, looked for a mirror in a quick glance around the bare cell, and then took her small handbag from the end of the bunk. "How do I get out?" she asked.

Sam filled his lungs with air and called for Pete.

All through the long afternoon, Sam sat quietly and lived over and over again the few brief minutes that had given him a new reason to live. He even permitted himself to hope that he would emerge from this whole experience exonerated and respected by everyone. He was immeasurably strengthened by the knowledge that she believed in him even though he stood accused of murdering her own father. And her faith would bring him through!

Then he remembered something else. The ripe figure of smirking Delores Purdy rose in his mind. The oceans of eternity separated her from the girl he had held that day. But Delores said he had seduced her. What would Duena think when she learned of *that?*

The dream castles which Sam had allowed himself to build split and crumbled into piles of arid and spiritless sand.

— *11* —

It was nearly dark when Virgil Tibbs drove the ancient car he had been loaned into the little filling station and garage operated by Jess the mechanic. The big man was working on a huge, air-conditioned Lincoln that was up on blocks in the rear of his garage.

"I need some gas, Jess," Virgil said, "and I think maybe I can give you your car back tomorrow."

"Leaving us?" Jess inquired as he started the pump.

"I think so," Tibbs replied, "but that's between you and me. Don't let it out."

Jess fitted the hose and began to feed gas into the tank. "I won't."

"Pretty fancy car." Tibbs nodded toward the Lincoln. "How come you're working on it?"

"Tourist car," Jess answered laconically. "The garage on the highway gets 'em, then they farm 'em out to me to fix. I'd like to get what they do for my work."

"They've got to pay their overhead," Tibbs pointed out, "and if they're on the highway, it must be a lot more."

Jess finished filling the tank. "Wait a minute," he said, and disappeared around the side of his shop. In three minutes he was back. "We figure on you eating with us," he announced flatly.

"Thanks a lot," Tibbs replied, "but I couldn't."

"I got a boy," Jess explained, "he's thirteen and he's

never seen a real live detective. I promised him."

Silently Tibbs got out of the car. A few minutes later he sat down to eat a modest meat-loaf dinner which was obviously being stretched for his benefit. At his right, Jess's son Andy watched his every movement until it was an embarrassment to eat. Finally, when the boy could contain himself no longer, he burst into speech. "Would you tell us about your first case?" he blurted, and waited with shining eyes.

Tibbs obliged. "It was a narcotics-smuggling problem. Somewhere in Pasadena little capsules of heroin were being transferred and sold. I was assigned to the case along with several officers."

"Were you a detective then?" the boy interrupted.

"No, I wasn't. But I had five years' service on the force and they decided to give me a chance. Then one day at a downtown shoeshine stand a man who was getting his shoes shined finished his newspaper and offered it to another man, who was waiting for service. The point was that the first man had on a new pair of shoes that didn't really need shining."

"How did you find that out?"

"I was the shoeshine man," Tibbs explained. "No one expected a Negro in a job like that to be a police officer."

"So if'n you'd been white, you couldn't of done it!" the boy burst out.

"I guess you're right," Tibbs agreed. "Though of course they'd have been caught sooner or later. But that was my real first case."

Andy turned to his food and tried the difficult job of eating without taking his eyes off the sensational guest who was actually sitting at his father's table.

When dinner was over, Tibbs excused himself, saying that he had urgent work to do. Since Jess's house was a short block from the garage, where he had parked,

Virgil said his good-byes at the door and began to walk down the darkened street to where he had left his car. His mind was reviewing carefully what he had to do next. It would not be pleasant and there would be problems. But, as he had learned many years ago, he would have to overcome problems if he wished to remain in his profession. It was harder here, that was all. This thought was still in his mind when a warning was flashed to him—too late.

He whirled to look into the faces of two men who had crept up behind him. As they lunged forward, he saw only that one of them held a heavy piece of wood in his hand and that he had it raised to strike. Tibbs braced himself, although he knew he was slightly off balance. As the man swung, Virgil leaped toward him and thrust his left shoulder into the man's right armpit. The heavy piece of wood snapped downward. As it did, Tibbs grabbed the man's forearm and at the same instant straightened his knees upward with all his strength.

The assailant's arm was trapped on top of Tibb's shoulder. His weight was thrust forward so that when Tibbs bent his back sharply forward, he had no choice but to ride over on Tibbs's back until he was upside down. In the same coordinated motion, Tibbs yanked hard at the attacker's trapped wrist. The man screamed as the back of his neck hit the concrete.

He was still falling when Tibbs let go of him and spun to face the other man, who was big but awkward, and had no weapon. Instead he doubled his fists and rushed in. Tibbs ducked under his first wild swing, grabbed his wrist, and spun around to the left. The big man, propelled by his own strength, twisted through the air and then fell heavily. Tibbs picked up the piece of firewood which so closely resembled the murder weapon. Then he looked up to see Jess's boy, attracted by the noise, staring at him with mixed fright and disbelief.

"Andy, go get your father as fast as you can. Then call the police and tell them to come here."

Andy ran off rapidly. He met his father halfway and poured out his message. A moment later, Tibbs was joined by the big mechanic, whose hands were opening and closing quickly as if waiting for the chance of combat. "They attacked me," Tibbs said. "Help me watch them."

Jess looked at the men. "Don't nobody move!" he commanded. The one who had attacked first was whining softly; his right arm lay twisted in an unnatural position. Andy came running back. "They're comin'," he reported. "I told 'em two men set on Mr. Tibbs and to get the doctor."

"Good, son," Jess said. "Now go get me a big tire iron. I don't need it, but it might be handy."

Andy took off, winded but eager to do as he was bid. He was back in seconds with the wicked tool. "It's a good thing we got that phone for emergency repair calls," Jess said to Tibbs.

Presently a siren could be heard wailing its way from the direction of the highway. Red lights came into view down the street and then the patrol car obeyed Andy's frantic signal to pull up to the curb. There were two uniformed men in it. Tibbs pointed to the figures which still lay quietly on the ground. "Assault with a deadly weapon," Tibbs said. "I'll prefer charges when we get to the station."

"*You'll* prefer charges?" one of the uniformed men questioned.

"I think he's Virgil," his partner said.

"I'm Virgil," Tibbs admitted. "Go easy with the man on the right. I think his arm's dislocated or broken."

When they reached the station, Gillespie was waiting for them in the lobby. "What happened?" he demanded.

"I had dinner with Jess the mechanic, the man you introduced me to," Virgil told him. "When I came out and was on my way back to my car, two men jumped me. One of them tried to club me with a piece of wood."

Gillespie seemed strangely pleased. "Bring 'em into my office," he ordered, and led the way. When the party had assembled as he directed, the chief sat behind his desk and viewed the two men for a long minute without speaking. Then he drew breath and made the room shake with the power of his voice. "Which of you two punks wrote me an anonymous letter?" he demanded.

There was no answer. The silence was broken by the buzz of the intercom. Gillespie flipped the key. "The doctor you sent for is here," the night man announced.

"Bring him in," Bill directed. A moment later, the desk man ushered in a tall, very slender, elderly Negro who carried a black bag. "I'm Dr. Harding," he said.

Gillespie pointed a long finger at the man who clutched his injured arm to his side. "Fix him up," he ordered. "When I heard two guys had jumped Virgil, I figured it was Virgil who got hurt so I told the desk man to call a colored doctor. Now you're here, you might as well go to work."

Dr. Harding ignored the insult and looked at his patient. "He'll have to lie down," he said. "Where can we put him?"

"Keep your hands off me," the man said. "I want my own doctor."

"Shut up," Gillespie barked. "I don't like people who write me letters and tell me what to do. We're providing you with a doctor like the law says."

134

"You won't last long in this town," the man retorted.

"Long enough," Gillespie said. "Take him in a cell and let the doctor work on him there."

The injured man was led away. Gillespie directed his attention to the other man. "All right, whose idea was this? Talk or you'll be in one heap of trouble."

"I ain't worried," the man told him. "I'll demand a jury trial. You know what that means."

"Sure, I know what it means," Gillespie told him. "So I'll tell you what I'm going to do. I'm going to call the paper and tell them how you and your pal jumped a little colored guy and that he beat the both of you up. Then you can have your jury trial."

"My story is that he and his big black pal jumped us with clubs," the man said, still unshaken. "We was minding our own business."

"Sure, in niggertown. You and your pal were on your way to a nice black whorehouse, just two respectable citizens, when you got mugged. Wise up; either way you lose."

"I ain't talkin'," the man maintained stubbornly.

Gillespie turned toward Tibbs. "You aren't a white man, but I guess you can fight," he conceded.

"The credit goes to the man who taught me," Tibbs said. "His name is Takahashi and he isn't Caucasian, either."

He turned toward the door. "I've got a job to finish and I'm getting near to the end. If you'll excuse me, I've got to get back to work."

To Tibbs's surprise, Gillespie got up and walked down the corridor with him. "Virgil," he said when they were by themselves, "I think you're smart enough to know you've got to get out of this town. Tonight you were lucky. Next time somebody may take a shot at you and that you can't duck. I'm giving you my advice—get out of here before I've got another murder on my hands. I'll tell them in Pasadena you did a good job for me."

"I'll get out, Chief Gillespie," Virgil answered, "but not until I have delivered Mantoli's murderer to you together with the proof of his guilt. I've got to do that first; perhaps you understand why."

"I won't be responsible," Gillespie said.

"That's all right," Tibbs acknowledged, and hurried through the lobby.

Duena Mantoli sat in the quiet of the early evening in the high lookout where, a few days before, Sam Wood had perched stiffly beside her. Now she was alone, looking out over the silent parade of the mountains trying to sort out her thoughts. She knew now that Sam Wood stood accused of seducing a sixteen-year-old girl, the daughter of an almost illiterate laborer.

Although she did not want to do so, she coldly compared herself to what she imagined the other girl to be. Then, with mounting shame, she saw herself standing on tiptoe in a jail cell to press her kiss on the lips of the man in whom she had found a sudden faith. That faith was gone now, which made her action, in retrospect, something cheap and vulgar. She folded her arms about herself and knew she had been a fool. It was hopeless to assume that breeding and what is called common decency could ever stamp out the basic instincts of sexual drive. Sam Wood was a big, strong man and he was unmarried. The girl, whoever she was, had been able to give him animal gratification.

Duena shuddered and tears of anger came to her eyes. She continued to sit there until Endicott, worried, came down to find her and take her back.

It was a little after nine on Saturday morning when Delores Purdy answered the doorbell. She preened herself for a moment first, because a girl could never tell who might be there. When she swung the door open and looked into the dark-skinned face of Virgil Tibbs, her mood changed abruptly. "Niggers go to the back door," she snapped.

"This one doesn't," Tibbs said. "I came to see your father."

"Don't you come in the door," she ordered, and then shut it in his face. A minute later, it was reopened by Purdy with an expression of profound distaste on his face. "Get away from here," he said. "We don't want you 'round."

"You don't have any choice," Tibbs told him, and calmly walked in. "I'm from police headquarters and I've come to talk to you and your daughter."

"I know who you are," Purdy snarled. "Now get out of here fast or I'll break you in two."

"If you try that," Tibbs retorted, "I won't be responsible for what happens to you. Two other guys tried it last night."

"Yeah, I heard tell. You and your pal jumped 'em at night and beat 'em up with tire irons. One of 'em is in the hospital."

"If you don't want to join him, shut up and sit down," Tibbs commanded. "I've had about all I'm going to take of ignorant back talk from you or anybody else. You came in and filed charges; "I'm here to talk about them."

"Ain't nothing more to say," Purdy said. "And no nigger is gonna sit down in my front parlor."

Tibbs walked in and sat down. "I came here to help you keep out of prison," he said.

Delores entered. "Pa, make him go away," she demanded.

"I'll go when I'm ready," Tibbs said. "Before I'm through talking to you, you'll both know that my coming here was the luckiest thing that could have happened to you."

"Niggers bring bad luck," Delores said.

"Mr. Purdy," Tibbs began, assuming a conference had begun, "you and your daughter came to the station and told us that somebody had done her wrong. Now it's our job to see that she's taken care of, that the man is punished, and that her reputation is protected."

"Sam Wood done her wrong," Purdy said.

Tibbs nodded as though he believed it. "So you told us. Of course, Chief Gillespie was very surprised; Mr. Wood has been on the force for several years and was always looked on as a very reliable man."

"He's in jail for murder." Purdy raised his voice almost to a scream.

Tibbs nodded again. "I know. I'm not going to give away any secrets but maybe there's a reason for it you don't know. I sat in a jail cell once for almost three weeks until the man who was in there too told me something the police wanted very badly to know."

"Black cop," Purdy threw it down like a curse.

"Now about the case of your daughter," Tibbs said quietly. "Whenever this happens and the man admits his responsibility, that's all there is to it. But Wood is a stubborn man. He won't admit that he did it. So now all the tests will have to be given. That is unless you can help me prove him guilty."

"You mean I got to tell it again?" Delores asked.

"What tests?" Purdy wanted to know.

"Well, in a case of this kind there is a lot that has to be done. The law says so. You see, it's hard for a man to prove he didn't have relations with a girl; the only way he can do it is through certain medical evidence."

"What's that?" Purdy asked. "She's my natural-born daughter."

Tibbs spread his hands. "Nobody doubts that," he said. "And everybody knows you're a respectable man. But because Sam Wood says he never even talked to your daughter, the cops are going to take some tests on her just to be sure."

"There ain't no test'll tell who done it to a girl," Delores protested.

"That's right," Tibbs agreed, "but there are tests that will prove a certain person *didn't* do it. Those are the ones you're going to have to take."

"Like what?" Purdy asked.

"Well, first they take a sample of her blood. That isn't so bad. They stick a needle in her vein at the forearm and draw out enough to fill some test tubes."

"I don't like needles stuck in me," Delores protested.

"Who's gonna do that?" Purdy demanded.

"The doctor will do that," Tibbs replied. "All these tests are done by doctors; nobody else will touch your daughter."

"They better not," Purdy said.

"Then, after that," Tibbs went on, "they have to make an examination to make sure that she was violated as she says. Also they have to find out whether or not she is going to have a baby."

Purdy sprang to his feet, his face twisted in a rage. "Ain't nobody gonna look at her secrets," he thundered. "I'll shoot the man who tries to look at her secrets. You get outa here."

Tibbs continued to sit still. "All I'm doing is warning

you," he explained. "You want to know these things before they come and do them when you're away, don't you?"

"Nobody's gonna look at her secrets," Purdy persisted.

"The only thing that will save her is if the man confesses," Virgil emphasized. "He says he's innocent, you filed charges, so the doctors have to examine her."

"Gillespie can stop it," Purdy said. "You'll see."

Tibbs shook his head. "He'd like to, of course, but the law won't let him. Wood can get a court order through his lawyer and then you have no choice." Tibbs locked his hands together and stared at them as he made his next statement. "Now I want to tell you something that's very important. But I don't want you to tell anyone I told you. I just don't want to see an innocent man like you framed and put into trouble."

"They can't do nothin' to me, I didn't do it." Purdy let his voice reach for hysteria. "I told you she's my own natural-born daughter."

"Of course she is," Tibbs said, putting sudden authority in his tone. "But suppose you get up in court and say that Sam Wood is the man who got her into trouble. Then suppose the doctor makes a mistake and says he isn't. That leaves you guilty of perjury, swearing falsely in court, and for that you can go to prison. That's what I want to warn you about and tell you how to protect yourself."

"Doctors don't make mistakes like that," Delores protested, but heavy strain showed in her voice.

"Sometimes they do," Tibbs said, "and juries believe them. Now suppose you tell me just how it happened, then I'll try to get Sam Wood to confess. If he does, you both have nothing to worry about."

"You mean then they'll leave us alone?" Purdy wanted to know.

"That's right," Tibbs told him.

He turned to his daughter. "Tell him," he ordered.

Delores wiggled in her chair and tried her utmost to look the violated virgin. Instead she looked more like a carnival Kewpie-doll.

"Well, he's always coming past here at night, peeking in the windows," Delores began. "I should of told my pa but I was kinda scared, him bein' a cop and all that. Then one night when Pa was out he come by and knocked on the door. Said he was on his way to work. He was askin' for names of girls who would like to be queen of the music festival. He said I was real cute and he wanted to put my name down for queen."

She stopped and looked up. Virgil nodded for her to go on.

"Well, he sweet-talked quite a bit and said even though he worked nights, he still saw a lot of people and could get me enough votes so's I'd win. Iffin I did, I'd win me a trip to New York. I don't remember too much after that. He gave me a drink he said wouldn't hurt me but would make me feel real good. He said I was the future queen and everybody would wish they was me. He said in New York I'd learn to sing and dance and maybe even be in the movies. He said he could make it all come true and that I oughta be real grateful to him....After that I don't remember so much except when he went away he said for me not to worry because he had been careful. Them's his words, he said he'd been careful."

Tibbs got to his feet. "You're sure it was Sam?" he asked. "I just don't want to make any mistakes that might hurt you."

Delores looked up, her face a mask. "It was Sam," she said.

Virgil Tibbs left the house and drove away. He went to the police station and put in a long-distance call to

Gottschalk, the missile engineer. Then he paid a visit to Harvey Oberst, who hated to be seen with a Negro but who remembered that this particular Negro had gotten him out of jail. Then he called on the Reverend Amos Whiteburn and talked to two small boys who were produced for his benefit. After that he returned to the police station and phoned a hotel in Atlanta. All this done, he called on two Negro residents of Wells and four white residents, two of whom refused to receive him. He also paid a visit to Dr. Harding. When at last he was finished, he was weary almost to exhaustion. He had had very little sleep and he was tired of battling opposition that was no fault of his. But at least he had his reward. He was ready now to talk to Bill Gillespie.

— 12 —

In the morning, after a bitter and restless night, Duena Mantoli arose to find that she had made up her mind. She took a long, refreshing shower. When she was through, she paused for a minute to look at herself in the glass. She knew that she was unusually pretty and she knew also that she worked hard to keep herself that way. Very well; physically she could at least match anything that wore skirts; the thing she must do now was to call upon another part of her heritage. It was time for her to use her brain.

She dressed and went down to breakfast. George and Grace Endicott were waiting for her. "We've heard from Eric," Grace told her as soon as she was seated, "and he has very good news. Two pieces of it. First of all, he's managed to get a very prominent conductor to save the festival for us."

"Who is it?" Duena asked.

"Eric wouldn't say; he said he wanted to suprise us when he gets here. The other good news is that the agency handling the ticket sales reports we are doing much better than they had expected."

"I'm glad to hear that," Duena said. She drank a glass of orange juice and then told them what was really on her mind. "You're going to think I'm crazy when I tell you this, but I'm going down to the city today to see Mr. Schubert. I want to talk to him."

"What about?" Endicott asked.

"I don't like the way things are going. Something's wrong. He's got a man in jail I happen to think is innocent. I don't understand why he hasn't been released on bail or else brought up for indictment, whatever the legal procedure is."

Grace Endicott took over. "I wouldn't, Duena. Frankly, neither you nor I are experts in these things and all we could do is get in the way of the people who are. It won't help matters and it might even hinder them."

Duena poured herself more orange juice and drank it. "You don't understand. Mr. Wood, the officer who was up here...that day...is in jail. He's not guilty, I know it. Don't ask me why now, but I know. That's why I want to see the mayor."

George Endicott picked his words carefully. "Duena, I think you're getting emotionally involved. Sit tight and let the men handle it. If Wood is innocent, he won't be in jail very long. And then there's Tibbs; he impresses me as competent."

"That won't help him much here," Duena retorted. Then she changed her tack. "Oh, well. Are you going down today?"

"Yes, this afternoon."

"Then may I come along for the ride? Maybe I can at least do some shopping."

Endicott nodded his consent to that.

Frank Schubert adjusted his posture in his chair, conscious of the challenging femininity of his visitor. He wondered how she had talked George Endicott into bringing her here, but it was evident that she had.

"Miss Mantoli," he began, "I'm going to be very truthful with you; in fact I'm going to give you some confidential information. Will you promise me to keep it strictly to yourself?"

"I promise," Duena said.

"All right. I don't know how much you know about the economy of the South, but certain areas have been very hard hit. Wells is one of them. We aren't on the main highway, only on an alternate route that perhaps one car in fifty chooses to take. That means that we lose a lot of tourist revenue. Agriculture is on the decline in this vicinity, industry so far has refused to move here, and putting it bluntly, both the city itself and many of the people in it are close to being on the rocks."

Duena, who was listening carefully, nodded.

"We realized—the council members and myself—that something would have to be done about it or we would be in a very serious situation. So George here came up with the music-festival idea. It didn't go over too well at first, but he convinced us that it would put us on the tourist map. If that were to happen, it would be a tremendous help. So, with some misgivings, we went ahead. I understand now that ticket sales are very good, so George appears to have proved his point.

"Now this brings up another matter, one that concerns you directly—or indirectly. The job of police chief came open and we had to fill it. None of the men on the force were anywhere near to being ready to step into the job. So we had an idea. We thought that if we advertised the opening, we might attract a good lawman who would take the job even at a very small salary, for the sake of the title and the experience. Then, when we got on our feet, we could raise his salary enough to keep him or else hire a replacement if we wanted to.

"Well, it worked out that our thinking, as far as it went, was correct. We had several applicants willing to work for the salary for the sake of the career advancement it would represent. One of them was Bill

145

Gillespie. Certain members of the council—and I'm mentioning no names—insisted on a southerner, who would at least do all he could to maintain our traditional race relationships. Someone from the North might shove integration down our throats long before we were ready to accept it and, if possible, make it work."

"So you hired Gillespie," Duena said.

"We did. His record looked very good, as much as we could hope for for what we had to offer. Personally, I will tell you in strict confidence that I consider we made a bad choice, but at least the certain council members I spoke of a moment ago were satisfied."

Schubert looked about him as if to make sure that no one else was within earshot. Then he leaned forward to make his words more confidential. "If he has the wrong man in jail, he will be out before very long, I'll promise you that. But you must understand there is strong evidence against him. Now I have talked to some of the council members, and I'm telling George here now that if Gillespie doesn't get this thing straightened out in the next few days, we're going to recall him. He's under contract, but there's a trial period and it isn't over yet. So don't worry, we'll handle that end."

It was a few minutes before four when George Endicott and Duena Mantoli left the mayor's office. They had received word that Eric Kaufmann was coming by early in the evening. When George Endicott had suggested staying down for a quiet supper and then picking up Kaufmann afterward, Duena had had her chance. It was still too early to eat but she had another idea. "I have to see Mr. Tibbs," she explained.

"I think you had better postpone that," Endicott advised. "If you went over there now you might make an inadvertent slip and that could be serious."

Duena looked up at him with an expression which combined disappointment and reproach; George Endicott suddenly decided that perhaps in his capacity as councilman he ought to exchange a few words with Bill Gillespie.

Arnold spoke through the bars to Sam Wood. "You've got another visitor." He swung open the door to admit Virgil Tibbs. The Pasadena detective walked in without an invitation and sat down on the edge of the hard bunk.

"Well, Virgil," Sam asked wearily, "what is it now?"

"I just wanted to tell you," Tibbs replied, "that I'm going in to see Gillespie as soon as he gets back here. When I do, I'm going to prove to him, so that even he can see it, that you're innocent. I think I can make him let you go."

Sam spoke without inflection. "Why don't you just give up and go home. I thought you were smart."

"I haven't finished my job," Virgil answered. "The world is full of a lot of people who never accomplished anything because they wouldn't see it through. I have two things left to do here: to get you cleared and out of here, and to deliver a murderer to Gillespie. Then I can go home."

"I wish you luck," Sam said. He didn't look at Virgil as he spoke.

"Before I go in to see Gillespie, I want to clear up a point or two with you," Tibbs said. "I'm pretty sure I know the answers, but the less I have to guess, the stronger my case is going to be."

Sam shrugged his shoulders. "What's on your mind?" he asked.

"On the night that we rode together on patrol, you made a slight change of route and you made it on purpose. At the time I didn't know why. I think I do now. You wanted to avoid going past the Purdy house, is that right?"

Sam showed some signs of life. "Virgil, I wish you wouldn't mess in this. I know you're trying to help, but..."

"Also," Virgil continued, "I think I know *why* you didn't want to go past the Purdy house that night."

"Have you been driving past there?" Sam asked suspiciously.

"No," Tibbs answered, "I didn't have to. Harvey Oberst told me all I needed to know the day he was here in the station."

He stopped then and there was silence for a while. Sometimes he found it best to let someone have the opportunity to collect his thoughts. He knew that Sam was thinking and that is exactly what he wanted him to do. Finally Sam broke the silence.

"Virgil, let's go back to the beginning. You've said several times I changed route on you that night. Why do you think so?"

"There's nothing to that," Tibbs replied. "The night we were together you detoured down a short stretch of dirt road. When I was waiting for you outside the diner a little after that, I noticed the dust the road had left on the car."

"That's not unusual," Sam interrupted.

"Granted, but the night you picked me up at the railroad station, there was no dust on the car. That means you couldn't have gone down that dirt road shortly before you picked me up."

"Maybe you just didn't notice the dust."

"I noticed. Besides, I had a hunch the car had been washed that afternoon, and I later checked with the garage that maintains the official cars. Even a light film of dust would have been visible."

"You mean when I arres— when I brought you in for questioning, you still took the time to notice how much dust there was on my car? You couldn't, you were a little too scared at that point, Virgil."

"No, I wasn't," Tibbs answered. "I simply kept my mouth shut until I knew what the score was. It was the only safe thing to do. But I kept my eyes open because I'm trained to do that."

"Well, for example, how do you know that it hadn't rained and settled the dust on that short stretch?" Sam persisted.

"I checked the weather-bureau records on that point."

Silence took over once more. Sam digested the information he had just been given and decided that to hold out any longer would be not only foolish but probably useless. Whether he liked to admit it or not, Tibbs knew his business. Then Sam reflected that at least the man whose race had created a barrier he had found almost impossible to climb was on his side. That was a comforting thought. He decided to give Tibbs his reward.

"So far," he admitted, "you're right."

"I wish you'd told me earlier, Sam," Tibbs said more easily. "It would have saved a lot of time—your time, I mean." To Sam's surprise Tibbs rose to his feet. "For your information, I had a little talk with Mr. Purdy and his daughter Delores. I scared them pretty well with the prospect of medical examinations to uphold her story, then I made a date for them to come in here late this afternoon for an 'examination.' I didn't say what kind. If I can get her to change her story in front of witnesses, then the charge against you goes out the window. When you've been proved innocent of that, the rest will be easier."

For the first time Sam felt the desire to cooperate.

"Virgil, maybe it would help if somehow you could find out who did knock her up. I know that's asking a lot."

"Thanks, Sam," Virgil replied. "I think I already know the answer.

When Bill Gillespie was told that Virgil Tibbs wanted to see him, he decided to keep Virgil waiting a few minutes just to keep him in his place. After what he considered a proper disciplinary period, he buzzed the intercom and said that he could come in.

Because of the delay, Tibbs walked into Gillespie's office at almost the exact moment that George Endicott escorted Duena Mantoli into the lobby of the police station. Endicott was edgy about the call, but he realized he had a determined girl on his hands and he preferred to have the interview with Gillespie take place when he could at least exercise some control. He stepped to the desk. "We'd like to see Chief Gillespie," he stated. "Is he free right now?"

Pete, knowing he was addressing a councilman and the wealthiest citizen of Wells, said, "You can go right in. Nobody's with him but Virgil."

They walked down the hall and George tapped on the side of the open door. Gillespie looked up, saw who it was, and said, "Come on in."

Then he stood up when he saw Duena also appear in the doorway. "Sit down, please," he invited after he had been introduced to the girl. "Virgil, run along and I'll talk to you some other time."

Virgil did not move to go. "What I have to say is fairly important, Chief Gillespie. Since Miss Mantoli and Mr. Endicott are here, perhaps it would be just as well if they heard it, too."

Gillespie raised his fist to bang it on his desk. Backtalk he would not take from anyone, least of all a man who stood on the wrong side of the color line. Endicott saw it and quickly spoke first. "This sounds interesting. With your permission, Bill, I'd like to hear what Mr. Tibbs has to say."

"So would I," Duena added.

Gillespie could see no way out. Inwardly vowing a quick and deadly reprisal the moment he had Tibbs alone, he accepted temporary defeat. "As you wish, Mr. Endicott."

They all sat down. "Before I begin," Virgil said, "I'd like to ask that Sam Wood be brought in here to listen." He looked at Gillespie. "Also Chief Gillespie may want to ask him some questions."

Fuming and cornered, Gillespie flipped his intercom and gave an order; a few moments later Sam Wood was ushered into the room. Gillespie nodded silently toward a chair and Wood sat down. With a second nod Gillespie dismissed Arnold, who had brought the prisoner in. Still holding down a dangerous inner pressure, he stared hard at Tibbs. "All right, Virgil, you'd better make it good."

Tibbs laced his fingers together and pressed them tightly. He stared at them for a second or two before he began speaking. "I'm going to start with the personality of a young woman, Delores Purdy." He looked up. "Miss Purdy is the daughter of a visibly retarded man whose intellectual level and education are both substandard. I haven't met her mother, but her family background, at the best, is lacking."

"I know all this," Gillespie snapped.

Tibbs waited a moment and then went on. "Delores Purdy is eighteen years old; she passes for sixteen so she will not be scoffed at in school for being two grades behind the point where she should be. The fact that

151

she is actually eighteen puts her over the age of consent, so any question of statutory rape is eliminated right there.

"Now Miss Purdy has one characteristic which has appeared on the police records quite clearly. She is an exhibitionist. For some reason she has the idea that her body is enchanting and likely to provide an unqualified thrill to anyone who sees it—anyone male, that is. It is fairly common in girls of her age who feel, in one way or another, that they have been deprived of social acceptance. They believe they can overcome this handicap by sensational conduct, irresistible to males."

He looked up to see how Duena was taking his words. She showed frank interest; so did the other three men. He went on. "The most common thing that happens is that a girl in these circumstances gives herself to a man in the hope of attaching him to her for the sake of her physical advantages. Sometimes it works, sometimes it simply brings about a further rejection.

"According to Harvey Oberst, who is a little older than she is, she displayed herself to him without his even asking for that favor. I believe this is so because of two supporting pieces of evidence. The first is her visit here to file a complaint against Mr. Wood. It is a serious matter to come into a police station to make an accusation against a popular and respected officer. But instead of being in the least upset, she had on figure-revealing clothes and wore her brassiere in such a way that it pushed her breasts up in an unnatural and highly conspicuous position. That is not the action of a modest girl who has been violated."

Tibbs paused and waited a moment, but none of his four hearers showed any signs of interrupting him.

"Now we come to the matter of Mr. Wood. On the

night of the murder, Mr. Wood drove his police car past the Purdy home. This was entirely consistent with careful performance of his duty; he had already covered almost every other part of the city and for him to patrol this area was both his privilege and his obligation. He went past a few minutes after three in the morning. He has not told me what took place at that moment, but I can guess. A few nights later, when I was riding with him, Mr. Wood pointedly avoided driving past the Purdy house; not knowing why, I jumped to the conclusion that he had something to conceal. My faith in him was shaken for a time; I was wrong, and for thinking that of him, I apologize."

"How did you know where the Purdys live?" Gillespie asked.

"Harvey Oberst mentioned it when I interviewed him here a few days ago, and I checked for myself with the records."

Gillespie nodded that he was satisfied.

"Now putting the pieces together as far as we have them, here is what happened as closely as I can reconstruct it. At some time in the recent past, Miss Purdy was indiscreet with a man of her acquaintance and ended up either pregnant or believing she might be. Who that man is is not important at the moment, except that she couldn't or didn't want to marry him. Believing herself to be 'in trouble,' she did what many young women have done—she looked around for someone to blame who would be unable to defend himself positively and who would be a more desirable temporary husband or source of obstetrical and child-care expenses. Fortunately this variation on the old badger game is thoroughly understood in police circles so that the unsupported word of a girl is seldom taken at its face value without some sort of supporting evidence.

Of course, Mr. Gillespie knows this well.

"Miss Purdy knew that Mr. Wood patrolled the city at night on the graveyard shift and therefore it could be believed that he had made one or more stops at her house during the year that the Purdys have lived in Wells. Secondly, she knew that he was unmarried and therefore might be trapped into marriage. Lastly, she was attracted to him, at least to a degree, as evidenced by the fact that she revealed herself to him at least once during his nightly rounds, probably in such a way as to make it appear an accident. It would be my guess that this had happened more than once, but not often enough to arouse the suspicion of a conscientious police officer." Tibbs looked at Sam Wood. "I don't want to embarrass you, Mr. Wood, especially in Miss Mantoli's presence, but can you confirm that?"

Sam took a moment to find the words. Then all he said was, "Yes."

"Now comes a matter of probability," Tibbs went on. "*If* Mr. Wood were guilty of accepting the attentions of such women, or inviting them, this tendency probably would have been visible at some time during the three preceding years that he has been guarding this city at night. This is not completely true, because people who have always led exemplary lives have been known to commit murder or run off with bank funds without warning. However, Mr. wood is a bachelor, with the right, therefore, to invite young women out in as great a variety as he chooses; if he had been inclined to take advantage of an unschooled girl, he probably would not enjoy the very good personal reputation that he has in Wells. No one knows a man's standing better than his bank, and the bank where he transacts business thinks very highly of Mr. Wood; they told me so.

"Summing up," Virgil said, taking a deep breath, "concerning the charge Delores Purdy made against Mr. Wood, I think it's a damn lie."

"Could you make her admit it?" George Endicott asked.

The intercom buzzed.

Bill Gillespie flipped the switch. "Mr. Purdy and his daughter are here to see you," the voice came through.

Gillespie carefully scanned the faces of the four people before him. "Bring them in," he instructed, "and bring a couple of chairs with you."

There was a tense quiet in the office while the footsteps of the Purdys could be heard coming down the hall. Everybody watched the doorway.

Delores came first. Her steps were short and slow. Her father's face was as hatchet hard as before, and the lines around his mouth seemed to have been etched even deeper. Arnold, who was behind them, came through the doorway sideways, juggling two chairs, which he set in position. No one spoke until he had left.

"Sit down," Gillespie invited.

Purdy nodded toward Tibbs. "Get him out of here," he ordered.

Gillespie appeared to grow taller in his chair. "He stays," he said, and motioned toward the chairs. The Purdys sat down.

"I ain't gonna talk with no nigger in the room," Delores announced.

Gillespie ignored her. "We have quite a bit of routine to put both of you through," he told the Purdys. "The medical part of it may take some time. Is there anything you'd like to tell me before we get started?"

There was a long silence. Gillespie leaned back and

155

his chair creaked under his weight. Then the room was quiet again.

Delores squirmed in her chair and smoothed her skirt with her hands. "I guess maybe I made a mistake," she said finally.

"You told us about that last time," Gillespie answered.

Delores waited for her slow mind to find the words she wanted. "I mean I guess maybe it wasn't him."

"You mean Mr. Wood?" Gillespie asked.

"Yeah, him."

Purdy cleared his throat and took the floor. "You see, Delores, she don't sleep so good at night sometimes. She seen the police car come past and she knowed who was in it. Then when she went to sleep after that she dreamed about him and that's just what give her the idea."

"You mean," the chief said, "your daughter saw Mr. Wood in the patrol car and then just dreamed that he had had relations with her?"

The muscles of Purdy's jaw worked before he answered. "Yeah, something like that," he said.

Gillespie tilted forward. "I find it pretty hard to believe a girl like Delores would dream so vividly about a thing like that that she would come down here and file a formal complaint. If she'd been a few months younger she could have put a man in danger of his life."

"Well, she ain't," Purdy snapped. "She's old enough to do as she pleases."

"Now I don't have to be examined, huh?" Delores asked.

"No," Gillespie answered. "If you and your father state here before witnesses that the charges you placed against Mr. Wood were in error, then there is no need for a physical examination."

"You couldn't now, anyway," Delores added.

Duena Mantoli made a slight noise, then the room was quiet again.

It was Virgil Tibbs who broke it. "You showed great courage in coming here this evening," he said to Delores. "Lots of girls wouldn't have been willing to do it."

"Paw made me," Delores admitted candidly.

"There's something you can do to help if you will," Tibbs went on. "It's more important than you might think. Could you tell us how you happened to dream about Mr. Wood?"

"I said she seen him come past and that put her mind to it," Purdy said angrily.

Tibbs ignored the remark and kept his eyes on Delores. Finally she took notice. She smoothed her skirt again and for the first time showed the beginning signs of embarrassment.

"Well," she said slowly, "he's a real OK guy. I never got to meet him, but I heard talk. He's got a real good job, steady, and a car, and I thought about him. I thought maybe he'd like me, especially 'cause I heard he didn't have no girl."

"I'm his girl," Duena said.

Sam Wood looked at her with wonder and disbelief.

Delores, too, looked at Duena. When she had finished, she turned listlessly back to face Bill Gillespie. She was inert, ready to topple whichever way she was pushed.

"He can't have my girl, he's too old for her," Purdy said.

Bill Gillespie made a decision. "Since you both came forward with a statement that clears Mr. Wood, as far as my department is concerned, we'll call it a closed incident. That doesn't mean that Mr. Wood won't sue you for defamation of character; I imagine he probably will."

"I don't want to sue anybody," Sam said.

Purdy turned toward his daughter. "We'll go home," he said, and rose. Delores got up after him. Then she turned and tried hard to smile at Sam. "I'm real sorry," she said.

Sam remembered he was a gentleman and got to his feet. So did Virgil Tibbs. George Endicott remained seated. With no further remarks, the Purdys filed out. It took a few moments after they had gone for the atmosphere to clear.

"Now what happens?" Gillespie asked.

Virgil Tibbs answered him. "We finish clearing Mr. Wood. Is there any other point you want settled before you release him?"

"Yes," Gillespie replied. "I want him to tell me how come he had six hundred dollars plus in cash to use in paying off his mortgage."

Tibbs spoke before Sam could. "I think I can answer that. The bank told you he had that amount in cash, but they didn't tell you what kind of cash."

"Cash is cash," Gillespie said.

"Not in this case," Tibbs replied. "When I asked about it, they told me the money was largely in coins—quarters, halves, and even nickels and dimes. There were some bills, too, but the largest one was five dollars."

The light dawned. "You mean he'd been hoarding it?" Gillespie asked.

"That's right," Virgil replied. "It wasn't the smart way because he could have deposited it at interest and earned around eighteen dollars a year. And his money would have been a lot safer. I am inclined to believe he has been saving what he could this way ever since he has been on the force in order to pay off his mortgage. Probably on the basis of a quota he set for himself."

"I tried to make it fifty cents a day," Sam explained.

"Actually you did a little better than that," Tibbs told him, "closer to four dollars a week. But why didn't you put it in the bank?"

"I didn't want to spend it. That was my mortgage money. I kept it by itself and I never took a nickel out of it until I paid for my home."

"Anyhow, I think that clears that one up," Tibbs said, speaking to Gillespie. "Is he a free man now?"

Gillespie looked at George Endicott before he answered. The spirit seemed gone out of him. "I guess so," he said.

"Then," Virgil said, "I want to ask you to restore him to duty immediately so he can make his regular patrol tonight."

"I'd like to spend a night at home first," Sam said.

"I think it's important that you drive tonight," Tibbs answered. "And if you don't mind, I'm coming with you." Tibbs turned to face Gillespie. "I'm going to give you a guarantee," he said. "Unless something radical happens, before morning Mr. Wood will arrest the murderer of Enrico Mantoli."

— *13* —

When Sam Wood walked through the lobby of the police station and out into the open air, he had the strong feeling that he had just lived through a bad dream. The extremes of anger, outrage, and hopelessness he had felt were all spent now and he was back exactly where he had been before it had all started. Except for one thing: he had held Duena Mantoli in his arms and she had kissed him. And in the presence of witnesses she had stated she was his girl.

Of course she wasn't, Sam knew that. She had said that simply to embarrass Delores Purdy and she had succeeded. For a few precious moments, Sam allowed himself to imagine that she had meant it. Then he snapped out of it and remembered it was time for dinner.

He drove to the café that offered the only acceptable steaks in town and ordered one. He felt he had it coming.

The manager came over to exchange a word with him. "I'm glad to see you, Mr. Wood," he said.

Sam knew exactly what he meant. "I'm glad to be here," he answered in the same vein. "Tell the cook to make that a good steak, will you?"

"I did," the manager said. "Say, I wanted to ask you something. Don't talk about it if you don't want to, but the whole town is wondering. What goes with this black cop you got working?"

"Virgil?" Sam asked. "What about him?"

"Well, how come?"

"He's a murder expert," Sam said. "He happened to be on hand and the chief put him to work. That's all."

"Must be pretty hard on you," the manager ventured.

"Not on me, it isn't," Sam answered shortly. "He's smart as hell and he got me out of a jam." Sam was instantly proud of himself for standing up for the man who had stood up for him.

"Yes, but he's a nigger," the manager persisted.

Sam put his hands flat on the table and looked up. "Virgil isn't a nigger. He's colored, he's black, and he's a Negro, but he isn't a nigger. I've known a lot of white men who weren't as smart as he is."

The manager made peace at once. "Some of 'em are smart, I know. One of them even wrote a book. Here comes your steak." The manager saw to it that it was served with gestures. He even personally brought the bottle of catsup. Then he told himself that Sam Wood should be excused for anything he said because he had just been through a hell of an experience.

When he had finished eating, Sam drove home and threw up the windows to clear out the musty air inside. He got out his uniform and checked it over. Then he took a shower, ran over his chin with an electric razor, and lay down to get some rest.

He remembered briefly Virgil's promise that he was to arrest a murderer that night. It seemed a little unreal as the desire for sleep grew on him. His mind went blank and he slept deeply until his alarm jangled at eleven.

161

Virgil Tibbs was waiting for him in the lobby of the police station when he got there. Sam checked in as he always did; the desk man struggled to pretend that nothing had happened. With his report sheet under his arm, and the keys to his patrol car in his hand, he nodded to Tibbs. "Let's go," he invited.

They set out together as they had once before. "Where to, Virgil?" Sam asked.

"You're doing the driving," Tibbs answered. "Anywhere you like. It doesn't make any difference to me. Only let's stay away from the Purdy place tonight. I don't want to go through that again."

Sam asked the question that had been in his mind for the last hour. "Do you think the murderer of old man Mantoli will be out tonight?"

"I'm almost sure of it," Tibbs replied.

"Then maybe we had better check up on the Endicotts, see that everything is all right."

"I'm sure she is," Virgil answered. "Go up if you like, but there is better reason to stay down here."

"Do you want to tell me about it now? I'm supposed to arrest the guy, you said."

"I'd rather not, Sam. If I did, you might betray something at the wrong time. Keeping something to yourself to the point where everything you say, every movement you make, is still just the same as though you didn't have that knowledge is very hard to do. Until the time comes, the fewer who know the better."

"Can't we do something about it now?"

Tibbs looked out the window. "Sam, without giving offense, would you trust me and let me handle it? I promise you you'll be there when it happens. In fact, I'm trying to arrange it so you will make the arrest."

"OK, Virgil." Sam was disappointed.

The night had never seemed so long. They talked

of California and what it was like on the Pacific Coast, where Sam had never been. They discussed baseball and prizefighting. "It's a tough way to earn a living," Tibbs commented. "I know some fighters and what they have to take is pretty rugged. It isn't all over when the last bell rings. When the cheering stops, if there is any, it's down to the dressing room, where the doctor is waiting. And when he has to sew up cuts over the eyes or in the mouth, it hurts like hell."

"Virgil, I've wondered how come there are so many colored fighters? Are they just better, or is it maybe easier for them?"

"If it's any easier I don't know how. I talked to a fighter once who had had a bout in Texas. He took an awful whipping although he fought hard; he was over-matched. Anyhow, when the doc came around to fix him up, the needle in his bruised flesh hurt so much he let out a yell. Then the doctor told him he'd presumed it didn't hurt him because he was a Negro."

Sam flashed back mentally to a conversation he had had with Ralph, the night man at the diner. It seemed to him it had been weeks ago. Actually it had been the night of the murder. "How about those two guys who jumped you?" Sam asked after a while. "I didn't hear what happened to them."

"A guy named Watkins, a councilman, got them off. He told me if I knew what was good for me I'd shut up about it, otherwise I would be booked for breaking the man's arm."

"Do you think Watkins hired them?"

"I hope so, because if he did, he'll have to foot the medical expenses for the guy who got hurt. There are supposed to be some others out looking for me now." Tibbs said it calmly, as though he were commenting that it might rain in the next day or two.

"I just hope they try it when I'm along," Sam offered.

"So do I," Virgil admitted quickly. "It won't be so easy next time. Judo is a good system but it can only go so far. After that you're licked and there's nothing you can do about it but take one or two out on the way down."

"Does anything beat judo?" Sam asked.

"Aikido is very good, especially for handling belligerent suspects when you don't want to do them any physical harm. The Los Angeles police use it extensively. In a real fight when the chips are down, then karate is the last word. A good karate man is a deadly weapon."

"Are there any in this country?"

Tibbs paused before answering. "Yes, I know some of them. A lot of the things you hear about karate aren't true, it doesn't ruin your hands, for instance. But as a method of protecting yourself, karate is the best thing there is in the way of unarmed combat technique. The training is severe, but it's worth it."

Sam swung the car down Main Street and let the soft purr of the engine blend with the stillness of the night. He watched the picket fence of parking meters go by and then he paused to draw up to the curb across from the Simon Pharmacy. "Is it safe to stop here tonight?" he asked.

"I think so," Virgil answered him. Sam touched the brake gently and let the car drift almost by itself over toward the curb. When he stopped, the wheels were an even two inches away from the concrete facing. He picked up his clipboard to write.

"We've got company," Virgil said.

Sam looked up, startled. Then he saw movement in the thick, silent shadows which filled the store entrance. A figure stepped out of the blackness and walked toward them. It was a very tall man, but he walked without making much noise. An instant later Sam recognized Bill Gillespie.

The police chief bent down and rested his forearms on the windowsill of the car. "How is it going with you guys?" he asked.

Sam found his tongue thick; it was hard to answer. "All right so far. Nothing unusual. Couple of lights on, but no indication of any trouble."

Gillespie reached down and pulled the rear door open. "I think I'd like to ride along for a while," he said. He climbed in and shut the door. "Not much room back here," he added as his knees pressed against the rear of the front seat.

Sam reached his left hand down and notched the seat forward an inch or two to make more room in back. "Where would you like to go?" he asked.

"I don't care," Gillespie said. "Virgil said he was going to point out the murderer to you tonight and I'd like to see him do it, that's all."

Sam stole a look at the silent man beside him. The realization had just come that for the first time in his police career he had a partner. And despite his color, Sam felt he could rely on him. Virgil could think and he could handle himself. Both might be necessary before the night was over.

Sam slipped the car into gear, crossed the highway, and entered the shantyville section of the city. He drove slowly and looked as usual for dogs that might be sleeping in the street. He saw one and made a careful detour.

The garage of Jess the mechanic was silent and dark. So was the little parsonage of Reverend Amos Whiteburn. There was a night light showing in the combination office and residence of Dr. Harding, who ministered to the physical needs of the colored citizens of Wells. The car bumped across the railroad tracks and started up the street that led to the Purdy house. Sam debated what to do. Then he went ahead; after what had happened, everything should be quiet tonight. The Purdy house was dark and still.

"There's an odd feeling to this time of night," Gillespie said.

Sam nodded his agreement. "I always notice it," he answered. "It's a miasma in the air."

"A what?" Gillespie asked.

"I'm sorry. A certain feeling, a kind of atmosphere."

"That's what I meant," Gillespie commented. "Don't the Purdys live around here somewhere?"

"We just passed their house," Sam told him.

He drove on another three blocks and then turned toward the highway. He slowed up for the stop that he always made even though the street was usually deserted at this hour. This time there was a car coming and he waited for it to pass. As it did so, the overhead street light outlined it enough so that Sam recognized it. It was Eric Kaufmann's, or one exactly like it.

Sam turned and followed in the direction of the diner. "I usually stop about now for my break," he explained.

"That's OK with me," Gillespie said.

Sam picked up speed and kept the car ahead of him in sight. As they neared the city limits, the other car slowed and turned into the diner parking lot. Sam slowed down and allowed Kaufmann enough time to get inside before he drove into the lot. Sam and Gillespie got out.

"What about Virgil?" Gillespie asked.

"I'll wait here," Tibbs said.

"What would you like me to get you?" Sam asked him.

"Nothing, I guess. If I think of something, I'll let you know."

Sam and Gillespie walked into the diner.

166

Eric Kaufmann looked up in surprise when they entered. Then he got to his feet to shake hands. "This is quite an unexpected pleasure," he said.

"For us, too," Gillespie added. "How come you're here at this hour?" It was a friendly question, but there was an undertone to it which suggested that Gillespie really wanted to know the answer.

"I just came in from Atlanta," Kaufmann explained. "I've gotten in the habit of driving at night. It's cooler that way and there's less traffic on the road."

"I see," Gillespie said as he sat down. "Any news?"

"Definitely," Kaufmann replied. "I've managed to line up a big-name conductor, one of the very best, to take over in Enrico's place. I'm not telling you who he is because I want George Endicott to be the first to know. And the ticket sales are excellent. You are going to have some real crowds here next month."

Sam sat down and wondered what to order. He motioned to Ralph, the counterman, to attend to the others while he thought about it. All that would come into his mind was the promise that tonight he would arrest a murderer. His shift was now almost half over and nothing yet gave signs of action. In a little while the daylight would come and when it did the mystery of the night would evaporate. Somehow it seemed to Sam that it would be too late then. The murderer had struck by night; it would have to be at night, or so it seemed, that he would be captured. He became an unreal entity, not a normal person who walks down the street and who looks like everybody else.

But how do you tell a murderer?

Sam ordered a root-beer float and toast, a ridiculous combination, he realized a moment later, but he waited while Ralph made it and then just looked at it as it sat in front of him. Then he heard a noise behind him.

Sam turned to see Virgil Tibbs standing just inside

the door. The Negro seemed pathetically weak at that moment, as though he was all too aware that he had ventured where he did not belong.

Ralph looked up and saw him. "Hey, you, there! Out," he ordered.

Virgil hesitated and came a cautious step or two more inside. "Please," he said, "I'm awfully thirsty. All I want is a glass of milk."

Ralph looked quickly at his guests and then back at Tibbs. "You can't come in here, you know that. Go back outside. When these gentlemen get through, maybe one of them will bring a carton out to you."

"I will," Sam offered.

Instead of retreating, Virgil walked farther into the forbidden room. "Look," he said. "I know you have rules down here, but I'm a police officer just like these gentlemen. I don't have any diseases. All I want is to sit down and have something like the others."

Sam drew breath to arbitrate. Virgil was "out of line" for the first time since he had known him and Sam was suffering acutely from secondary embarrassment. Then, before he could speak, Ralph walked around the end of the counter and over to where Virgil was standing.

"I heard about you," Ralph said. "You're Virgil and you don't come from around here. I know about you. For the sake of these gentlemen I don't want to get rough, but you've gotta leave. If my boss ever hears that I let you walk in the door, he'll fire me for sure. Now please go."

"Why?" Tibbs asked.

Ralph's face flushed and his temper snapped. "Because I told you to." With these words, he put his hand on Virgil's shoulder and pushed him around.

Tibbs whirled on the balls of his feet, seized Ralph's extended arm with both hands, and pulled it behind him in a painful hammerlock.

Sam could stand no more; he was on his feet and came forward. "Let him go, Virgil," he said. "It isn't his fault."

Virgil Tibbs seemed not to hear the remark. His hesitant manner had vanished and on the instant he was all business.

"Here he is, Sam," he said. "You can arrest this man for the murder of Enrico Mantoli."

— 14 —

It was a dirty, hot dawn which streaked the sky. What colors there were were smoky and the beauty that often comes with the first light of day was not there. Virgil Tibbs sat waiting in the detention room of the police station, reading another paperback book; this one was *Anatomy of a Murder*.

After almost three hours, the door of Gillespie's office opened. There was the sound of footsteps and then the clanging of a cell door. A few moments later, the big man who headed the Wells police department came into the detention room. He sat down and lighted a cigarette. Tibbs waited for him to speak.

"He signed a confession," Gillespie said.

Tibbs put his book down. "I was sure you could do it," he said. "Did he implicate the abortionist?"

Gillespie looked slightly startled. "You seem to know all about this, Virgil. I'd like to know how you doped it all out."

"Where's Sam?" Virgil asked. It was the first time he had used Wood's first name in Gillespie's presence.

Apparently Gillespie didn't notice it. "He went back out on patrol. Said it was his job."

"He's an exceptionally conscientious officer," Virgil said, "and that means a great deal. With the music crowds coming here soon, you will be needing more help."

170

"I know it," Gillespie said.

"I was thinking that Sam would make a good sergeant. The men could look up to and respect him and Sam is ready for the job."

"Are you trying to run my department for me, Virgil?" Gillespie asked.

"No, I was just thinking that if you did decide on something in that direction, Sam would probably be very grateful to you. Under those circumstances I think he might forget all about the recent inconvenience he went through. Pardon my bringing it up."

Gillespie said nothing for a moment. Tibbs waited and let him take his time. "How long ago did you know it was Ralph?" the chief asked finally.

"Not until yesterday," Tibbs said. "I've got a confession to make, Chief Gillespie: I almost bungled this one beyond recovery. You see, up until yesterday I was hotly in pursuit of the wrong man."

The phone rang. The night desk man answered and then called to Gillespie. "It's for you, Chief," he said.

Gillespie rose to his feet and went to see who was calling at a little after seven in the morning. It was George Endicott.

"I called to ask when you would be in," Endicott explained. "I didn't expect to find you at this hour."

"You're an early riser," Gillespie said.

"Not normally. Eric Kaufmann called with the news that you and your men have caught Enrico's murderer. Please accept my very sincere congratulations. I understand you made the arrest personally. That was certainly a fine piece of work."

Gillespie remembered some of the resolutions he had made. "The actual arrest was made by Mr. Wood," Gillespie said. "I was there, that's all. My part came later when I questioned him until he broke down and confessed."

"I still can't believe you were there by accident," Endicott said.

The chief drew a deep breath and did what he had never done before. "You will have to give credit to Virgil; he had a lot to do with it."

Now that it was over, it hadn't been so bad. And Endicott was from the North, which made it easier still.

"Listen, I've talked to Grace and Duena. Although it may be a bit out of place so soon after Enrico's death, we want to have a quiet gathering here tonight. I hope you can arrange to join us."

"I'd be glad to."

"Fine, and will you please ask Sam Wood and Virgil Tibbs? I'm sure you'll see them."

That was a little harder to take, but Gillespie made the grade. "I'll tell them," he said.

When he hung up, he reflected that he had met two challenges and had defeated them both. He might as well make it three in a row. And if anyone in the station said anything about it, he could and would deal with them. He walked into the detention room. He looked at Virgil Tibbs and held out his hand.

Tibbs rose and took it.

"Virgil," Gillespie said, "I want to thank you for the help you've given us. I'm going to write a letter to Chief Morris and thank him for your services. I'm going to tell him you've done a fine job."

Gillespie let go of the first Negro hand he had ever clasped. He looked at the man behind it and saw, to his sudden surprise, that his eyes were moist.

"You're a man to be admired, Chief Gillespie," Tibbs said. His voice shook a very little.

Then it was that Gillespie recalled a famous quotation. He knew it because he had hated it; now, however, it could be of service to him.

"Thank you, Virgil," he said. "You're a great credit

to your race." He paused. "I mean, of course, the human race."

At seven-thirty that evening, Bill Gillespie picked up Sam Wood and Virgil Tibbs at the police station in his personal car. The two men climbed in. Tibbs sat in back.

There was little conversation as they drove up the mountain to the Endicott house; none of them had had very much sleep, but the summons to the gathering had to be obeyed. Gillespie wondered how he would feel at a social function where a Negro was a guest.

When they arrived, Grace Endicott met them at the door and led them into the big living room, Gillespie first, Sam next, and Virgil bringing up the rear.

The room was comfortably full. Eric Kaufmann was there, Jennings the banker and his wife, Duena Mantoli, and the Schuberts.

Sam Wood was vaguely aware of them all; he was acutely aware of Duena, whose beauty tonight almost literally took his breath away. He stood awkwardly in the middle of the floor, looked at her, and told himself once more that he had held this girl in his arms, and that she had kissed him. Vivid as the memory was, it was clouded with a veil of unreality.

George Endicott called for order. When it grew quiet and everyone was seated, he took the floor. He held a drink in his hands, which he looked at as he spoke. "This is a rather strange affair," he said, "but Grace and I wanted you all to come because, on top of crushing misfortune, we have many things to celebrate. We have a conductor for our festival; you all know now who he is. Our tickets are already almost sold out. The orchestra is in rehearsal. Mr. Kaufmann conducted the session yesterday and he tells me that our concerts are going to be of very high quality. So I want to announce that I am asking Mr. Kaufmann if he will favor us by appearing as conductor on at least one of our programs."

There was a little ripple of applause. Kaufmann colored and recovered himself. "I'd be proud to," he replied.

"Next, we have been looking around for a suitable name for our outdoor theater. In recognition of the fact that it was one man's energy, ability, and enthusiasm that made it possible, the trustees voted this afternoon to name it the Mantoli Bowl."

Everyone looked at Duena; she put her face in her hands and said nothing.

"I'm sure Duena will consent to dedicate it for us on opening night," Endicott went on. "Now we come to the third matter, the way in which our police force, augmented by the abilities of a most unusual man, found and arrested the person responsible for the disaster that overtook us. I don't know how this piece of work was done; I wish somebody would tell me. That is, if this is the proper time and place."

"I'd like to know, too," Frank Schubert seconded.

"Chief Gillespie?" Endicott invited.

In a moment of rare clarity, Gillespie saw there was only one thing he could do. He couldn't tell the story because he didn't know it. To confess ignorance at this stage of the game was unthinkable. And he realized fully that if he passed the credit to the place where it belonged, his own standing would grow as a result.

"Mr. Wood and Virgil made up the team who tracked him down," he said, keeping his voice moderated. "I suggest you ask them about it."

That, Gillespie thought, should square him with Sam for some time to come.

George Endicott looked at Sam. "Mr. Wood?" he said.

174

"Ask Virgil," Sam replied with genuine humility. "He did it."

"Mr. Tibbs." Endicott looked over to where the quiet Negro sat by himself. "You have the floor. I understand you are leaving us later tonight. Please don't go without telling us the rest."

Tibbs looked at Gillespie. "Go ahead, Virgil," the chief said.

"This is extremely embarrassing," Tibbs said. He looked as if he meant it.

"There's no need to be that modest," Endicott encouraged him. "I know your reputation on the Coast. A successful investigation is nothing new to you."

"It isn't that," Tibbs replied, "it's the fact that I can't conceal any longer how badly I bungled this one. It was only a stroke of pure luck that saved the day and I can't take any credit for it."

"Suppose you let us judge," Jennings invited.

Virgil took a deep breath. "In any murder investigation, one of the first things to do is to establish the motive for the crime if it is at all possible. When you find out who might benefit from the death of the victim, you have at least a point from which to start. This is assuming that there is no clear-cut solution which is relatively easy to track down.

"When Chief Gillespie arranged for me to stay here and assigned me to this case, I learned certain things from the physical evidence at hand and then went to work to establish the motive. Now I'm afraid I'm going to shock you all and Mr. Kaufmann especially. I doubt if he will ever forgive me. You see, for several days I thought he was guilty and I worked hard to prove it."

Tibbs looked up at the young conductor, whose face was a study. Sam Wood looked at him, too, and decided he couldn't tell what the man was thinking. But Sam was not surprised; he himself had been thinking about

175

Eric Kaufmann, though he couldn't exactly say why.

"You see," Tibbs continued, "Mr. Kaufmann had an immediate and powerful motive: Maestro Mantoli's tragic passing placed him in direct line to take over the music festival and both the fame and financial rewards that would result. Many men have killed for less than that. I might add that he disproved this motive completely by his energetic and successful work to secure a replacement conductor of established reputation on short notice.

"At that point Mr. Kaufmann was a suspect and no more. Then, on my first visit here, he happened to remark in my presence that Maestro Mantoli had been 'struck down.' The papers were not yet out, and having supposedly come directly here from out of town, he would have had no way to have known that Maestro Mantoli had been literally struck down. He might have been shot, or poisoned, or any number of things. So I interpreted his remark as indicating guilty knowledge and he at once became my number-one candidate for investigation. What I failed to do was to recognize that 'struck down' is a fairly common figure of speech and not necessarily a literal one."

"Is this too much for you?" Grace Endicott asked Duena, who was beside her. Duena shook her head without taking her eyes off Tibbs.

"Then came the matter of the cherry pie," Virgil continued. "When I checked up on Mr. Kaufmann's whereabouts on the fatal night, I learned that he had arrived in Atlanta at a time that could not be definitely established. And he had remarked to the elevator operator in the hotel where he was stopping that he had eaten a late dinner and questioned the wisdom of cherry pie at that hour. This sounded like a manufactured alibi to me for several reasons. One of them was that there was no proof that he had stopped to eat a full meal, but by claiming to have done so, he automatically added an hour to the time he was presumably in the city. Cherry pie at three in the morning, or something around that hour, is definitely unusual, I didn't believe he would have done it. Lastly, his mentioning it so obviously to the elevator man suggested to me he was doing so deliberately so that the man would recall the conversation later if asked. Mr. Kaufmann had no way of knowing that the night man at the hotel would not be able to be reasonably exact about the time of his arrival. By now I was convinced I knew my man, and I went after him with a vengeance."

"The way you put it, I can't blame you a bit," Kaufmann said. "I happen to be inordinately fond of cherry pie, but there is no way you could know that."

"You're extremely generous, sir," Virgil said to him.

"Go on, please," Duena asked.

"To continue confessing my sins," Virgil picked up again, "as soon as I was fixed on Mr. Kaufmann, I promptly failed to notice what was going on about me."

"The devil you did," Sam Wood interrupted. "You noticed how much dust there was on my car and made a considerable point of it."

Bill Gillespie would not be outdone. "You noticed that Harvey Oberst was left-handed," he added.

"Yes, but the important things I missed completely," Tibbs said. "While I was chasing Mr. Kaufmann, everything that actually concerned the case was taking place in a totally different direction. I kept trying to pin Mr. Kaufmann down and made a fatal mistake. I tried to make the evidence fit the suspect instead of the other way around. That sort of thing is inexcusable."

"Go on with the story," Grace Endicott invited.

"I'll finish my confession by saying that I went after the murder weapon and eventually it was delivered to me." Tibbs took another deep breath and then plunged

177

into the statement he felt he had to make. "It was discovered at the edge of the concert bowl, and while it did not point directly, it suggested Mr. Kaufmann again. I had, I thought, considerable evidence, but none of it would jell enough to hold water for five minutes in a court of law. The more I looked, the less I could find to aid my case because Mr. Kaufmann was, of course, entirely innocent.

"When Harvey Oberst was brought in on suspicion, I learned from him that there was a girl in Wells of the kind who makes trouble for almost everyone she contacts—Delores Purdy. I stored the fact away, but had no idea that the whole thing actually revolved around her. Then Ralph, the diner man, seriously accused an innocent and responsible missile engineer who simply happened to be driving through the city. It was extremely thin grounds for suggesting an arrest; it looked more like an attempt to muddy the waters, as indeed it was. So for the first time I began to wonder about this young man. But I saw no link between him and Delores Purdy."

"Was there one?" Duena asked.

Tibbs nodded. "Mr. Purdy works nights. Ralph knew about Delores and began to call on her when her father wasn't there. Mrs. Purdy apparently paid little attention to her children and cared less. Ralph and Delores had much in common. They were both unschooled, prejudiced, and of a low level of intelligence. And they were both in search of what they considered thrills. About six weeks or two months ago they became intimate; within the past few days Delores believed herself to be pregnant and when Ralph came to see her, she told him of her supposed condition and demanded that he help her.

"Ralph was frightened; he believed Delores to be sixteen and he knew enough to realize that was under

178

the age of consent. And he feared her father. So, like an unlimited number of others like him, he began frantically to look around for a way out. He knew that it would be hard to find a reputable physician to perform an abortion for him, but he thought that he could find one somewhere who would do it for him if he had enough money.

"I begin to see the light," Mayor Schubert commented.

"While Ralph was doing this, Delores had an idea of her own. Ralph was not much of a catch, but she thought she knew a man who would be."

Duena Mantoli, whose composure remained unshaken, looked across at Sam Wood. To Sam it was like an electric shock; he took a good hold on the arms of his chair and tried to compose the expression on his face.

"Almost every night Mr. Wood patrolled past her house, often at about the same time, since it was on his way to the diner, where he customarily stopped for a short break. She arranged, therefore, to allow Mr. Wood to see her naked. She felt confident that he would take notice and probably stop to speak to her, possibly to warn her that she was visible from the street. In either event, she felt that her physical charms, when revealed that way, would be irresistible. Once Mr. Wood had compromised himself with her, she could claim him to be the father of her child and expect thereby to take a considerable step up the social ladder. But Mr. Wood was both intelligent and morally responsible: he obviously realized fully that if he even stepped to the door to caution her, he would place himself in jeopardy, so he very wisely drove on and her little plan fell flat."

Sam Wood discovered that everyone was looking at him. *He* knew he had not thought it out quite that way, but there was clearly no point in saying so. At least he had behaved himself as he was credited with doing. He kept his breathing even and his mouth firmly shut.

"Then the thing happened that finally forced me onto the right track; Chief Gillespie, on the basis of some evidence which he himself had uncovered, arrested Mr. Wood on suspicion of murder. Now my prime objective was no longer to track down Mr. Kaufmann, but to prove Mr. Wood's innocence and get him out of jail. Here Miss Purdy came to my rescue; believing Mr. Wood to be in trouble, she immediately accused him of intimacies with her, feeling that he was in no position to protest."

"A nice girl," Jennings commented.

"Yes, but there are lots like her," George Endicott added. His wife nodded her silent agreement.

Virgil went on. "Mr. Wood provided me with a clue that pointed to the Purdy house and I began to take an awakened interest in that young woman. Thanks to Chief Gillespie's fast thinking, I listened in on a conversation that he had with her and her father; in the course of that talk she stated flatly that Mr. Wood used to call on her evenings *on his way to work*. That wasn't so, of course, but at that point the lights went on; there was one other person who went to work at that hour and a far more likely candidate for the doubtful distinction of being her boyfriend. Then I remembered how Ralph had tried to involve a clearly innocent man in an almost idiotic way.

"Now the pieces fell together fast. I checked and found six people who had seen Mr. Wood on his rounds on the night of the murder; the four of them who would talk to me in combination gave him a reasonably sound alibi. I found these people, incidentally, by calling at the houses where I had noticed lights on when I had covered the route with Mr. Wood in his patrol car.

People who get up in the small hours of the night often do so reasonably regularly and quite a few of them had noticed the police car on its rounds.

"Then I finally realized two more very important facts: the person who placed Maestro Mantoli's body in the middle of the main highway had to have an intimate knowledge of the probable traffic at that hour; Ralph met that qualification. And I saw the significance of the fact that it was a blazing hot night."

"You mean the weather had something to do with this murder?" Frank Schubert asked.

"Definitely, in two different ways. Both of them tended to give Ralph a very good alibi which he himself hadn't in any way planned. As soon as I remembered the heat of the night, a tremendous objection to Ralph disappeared and I knew that this time I had my man. I knew the motive, I had established opportunity, and as an individual he fitted perfectly into the pattern of conduct of the murderer."

"Exactly what did he do?" Endicott asked.

"He left early for work in order to see Delores. She made it clear that he must either 'take care of her' or face the consequences. All he thought he needed to escape from his predicament was money, but he had no savings and his salary was totally inadequate. He was cornered, or thought he was."

"But the girl really wasn't pregnant at all," Duena contributed.

"That's right," Tibbs said. "How did you find out?"

The girl looked at him. "The day I met her. Her relief was so evident it stuck out all over. She didn't want anything from anybody, only to be left alone. And she said she couldn't be examined."

"Go on," Gillespie said to Tibbs.

"On that night Ralph drove up the highway on his way to work thinking what to do. He decided he would

181

have to rob somebody and the question was who. A few minutes before, Mr. Endicott had dropped Maestro Mantoli at his hotel, which is second rate and not air-conditioned. Excited and enthusiastic about the music project, the Maestro probably realized he couldn't sleep immediately, and decided to take a short walk. Do you recall my asking if he was likely to make such impulsive decisions? At the same time I inquired if he was able to make friends quickly and easily, and if he would be likely to discount someone because he was of a real or imagined lower social status than himself."

"And I told you he was impulsive and met people almost eagerly," Duena said.

"You did. Then I saw how it happened. Ralph, coming up the street in his car, saw and recognized the Maestro; his appearance was very distinctive, at least in this city. Here, Ralph thought, was opportunity. He offered the Maestro a ride and Mr. Mantoli accepted.

"When I was first told the murder weapon had been found at the edge of the music bowl, I assumed that helped to implicate Mr. Kaufmann. I was totally wrong. Ralph said he had not seen the bowl and Maestro Mantoli offered to show it to him. He wanted to see it again himself, for that very evening plans for the festival had been settled.

"They drove to the bowl—Maestro Mantoli for the reasons I just stated, Ralph to rob him of enough money to solve his crisis. They got out at the edge of the bowl and stood looking over the setting. The spectators—or auditors is probably the word—will have to sit on logs for the first season at least. The last rows had just been put down and trimmings were scattered all about. Ralph picked up a piece of wood, and tried to think of the best way to use it. Then he had the wild idea that he would stun the Maestro and later claim that they had both been jumped from behind by persons unknown.

182

When he delivered the fatal blow, he intended it to be much less."

"Then it was...partly an accident?" Duena asked.

"Yes, assault with a deadly weapon and manslaughter, but not first-degree murder."

"I'm almost glad," the girl said quietly.

"When the Maestro slumped to the ground, unconscious, Ralph panicked. His first impulse was an honorable one, to get the man he had just injured to a doctor. He was in a cold sweat now, and terribly afraid. He carried the Maestro the few steps to his car, put him inside, and drove back to town. As he neared the center of the city he finally realized what he had done. He stopped on a side street, took out his victim's wallet, removed enough money to solve his first problem, and then left the body in the middle of the highway, with the wallet nearby. Then he drove quickly to the diner and reported late for work, which he regularly did two or three times a week."

"But why in the middle of the highway?" Grace Endicott asked, wide-eyed.

"He believed a hit-and-run driver would be blamed. That was a major clue, of course, the location of the body, but I didn't see the point for some time."

"And the temperature?" George Endicott added.

"Oh, yes, that did two things for Ralph: first it kept down the traffic to almost nothing and delayed the discovery of the body."

"Wait a minute," Frank Schubert interrupted. "How about that engineer who drove through?"

"While he was here no one asked *him* the exact time he had passed through the city. Ralph said it was forty-five minutes before Sam found the body, a statement Gottschalk didn't question because he didn't know when the body was found. He came through while Ralph was robbing his victim. Ralph noticed the unusual car and when the man stopped at the diner on his return trip, Ralph called the police department, hoping that Gottschalk would be arrested for hit-and-run."

Grace Endicott shook her head. "What a dreadfully warped mind that boy must have. I can't conceive of it. He's like an animal."

"The rest about the hot night," Gillespie prompted.

"Oh, yes, the unusual temperature gave Ralph a totally unexpected alibi. When the intern who came with the ambulance fixed the time of death, he did so in the usual manner, by estimating how much body heat had been lost. But he failed to allow for the unusual temperature and therefore was considerably off on his estimate. The hot night had literally kept the body warm. It wasn't until that major objection could be overcome, Ralph's apparent alibi, that I could be sure he was the man."

Tibbs looked suddenly very weary. "That's about all," he concluded. "I came into his diner and asked for a *glass* of milk. If I had said 'carton' he might have given it to me. The idea of my using a glass disturbed him and when I made a scene about being allowed to eat there, he was aroused to the point where he put hands on me. Then I was able to grab him; I shouldn't have done it that way, but I wanted the satisfaction. He so clearly despised me because of my ancestry, and considered himself so totally superior, I wanted to teach him a very important lesson. It was childish, I admit."

Bill Gillespie drove Virgil Tibbs to the railroad station. After he parked the car in front of the platform, he got out and picked up Virgil's suitcase. Tibbs understood and let him do it.

Gillespie led the way onto the train side of the platform and put the case down before the single bench that offered limited comfort to those who had to wait.

"Virgil, I'd like to stay with you, but frankly I'm dead for sleep," Gillespie said. "Do you mind if I go on?"

"Of course not, Chief Gillespie." Tibbs waited a moment before he spoke again. "Do you think it would be all right if I sat out here? It's a very nice night."

Gillespie knew without looking that the bench was marked WHITE. However, it was past midnight and the station was deserted.

"I don't think it would make any difference," he answered. "If anybody says anything, tell 'em I told you to."

"All right," Tibbs said.

Gillespie took two steps away, then he turned. "Thanks, Virgil," he said.

"It was a pleasure, Chief Gillespie."

Gillespie wanted to say something else, tried, but couldn't. The man before him was black and the moonlight accentuated the contrasting whites of his eyes.

"Well, good night," he substituted.

"Good night, sir."

The chief thought of shaking hands with him, but decided not to. He had done it once and that had made the point. To do it again now might be just the wrong action to take. He walked back to his car.

FINE MYSTERY AND SUSPENSE
TITLES FROM CARROLL & GRAF

☐ Ambler, Eric/BACKGROUND TO DANGER	$3.95
☐ Ambler, Eric/A COFFIN FOR DIMITRIOS	$3.95
☐ Ambler, Eric/JOURNEY INTO FEAR	$3.95
☐ Brand, Christianna/TOUR DE FORCE	$3.95
☐ Brand, Christianna/DEATH IN HIGH HEELS	$3.95
☐ Brand, Christianna/GREEN FOR DANGER	$3.95
☐ Carr, John Dickson/THE DEMONIACS	$3.95
☐ Carr, John Dickson/THE GHOSTS' HIGH NOON	$3.95
☐ Carr, John Dickson/THE WITCH OF THE LOW TIDE	$3.95
☐ Collins, Michael/WALK A BLACK WIND	$3.95
☐ Fennelly, Tony/THE CLOSET HANGING	$3.50
☐ Gardner, Erle Stanley/DEAD MEN'S LETTERS	$4.50
☐ Gilbert, Michael/OVERDRIVE	$3.95
☐ Graham, Winston/MARNIE	$3.95
☐ Griffiths, John/THE GOOD SPY	$4.95
☐ Hughes, Dorothy B/RIDE THE PINK HORSE	$3.95
☐ Hughes, Dorothy B/THE FALLEN SPARROW	$3.50
☐ Kitchin, C.H.B./DEATH OF HIS UNCLE	$3.95
☐ Kitchin, C.H.B./DEATH OF MY AUNT	$3.50
☐ Pentecost, Hugh/THE CANNIBAL WHO OVERATE	$3.95
☐ Queen, Ellery/THE FINISHING STROKE	$3.95
☐ 'Sapper'/BULLDOG DRUMMOND	$3.50
☐ Stevens, Shane/BY REASON OF INSANITY	$5.95
☐ Symons, Julian/THE BROKEN PENNY	$3.95
☐ Symons, Julian/BOGUE'S FORTUNE	$3.95
☐ Westlake, Donald E./THE MERCENARIES	$3.95

Available from fine bookstores everywhere or use this coupon for ordering.

Carroll & Graf Publishers, Inc., 260 Fifth Avenue, N.Y., N.Y. 10001

Please send me the books I have checked above. I am enclosing $_____
(please add $1.25 per title to cover postage and handling.) Send check
or money order—no cash or C.O.D.'s please. N.Y. residents please add
8¼% sales tax.

Mr/Mrs/Ms _____
Address _____
City _____ State/Zip _____
Please allow four to six weeks for delivery.